Stiletto SINS

KRIS BUTLER

Stiletto Sins
The Order Duet: Book One
By: Kris Butler

First Edition: July 2022
Published by: Incognito Scribe Productions LLC
Kris Butler

Proofreading: © 2022 by Owlsome Author Services
Formatting: © 2022 Incognito Scribe Productions LLC
Cover Design: © 2022 Incognito Scribe Productions LLC

✾ Created with Vellum

Stiletto SINS

KRIS BUTLER

Contents

Blurb

I didn't belong.

Not with the things I'd done. Not with my past.

To move forward, I needed to finish what I'd started all those years ago. I had to face him. My only barrier to the life I wanted was me, and it was time to face the sins of my youth instead of running.

Except now, I had to run.

My family wouldn't understand and I knew this would hurt, but I was out of options. If I didn't do this now, I'd always be wondering, waiting for him to strike. It was time for me to strike first.

So, I would be selfish just this once and find him, take him down and make him pay.

At one time, he'd been my salvation, until he became my damnation. My sins were dark, my spirit broken, but I was no longer *weak*.

It was time I remembered who I'd been. It was time I returned to Oblivion. This time, my stilettos wouldn't just be sinful. No, this time, they'd be *deadly*.

Join Finley, Asa, Cohen, and Milo in this spy-esque why-choose romance that will contain dark themes. Please read the trigger warning before reading. This is book 1 in a duet and intended for readers 18+ and older due to adult situations and content. This is a spin-off of The Council Series, but it isn't necessary to read first. Some characters will crossover, enriching the experience, but aren't required to know in order to enjoy the story.

Foreword

This book has sexual scenes meant for adults. It is a reverse harem romance that might include MM. The steamy scenes are steamy. This book uses the F-word on occasion, though, Fin has her own way of cussing.

This book deals with triggers of suicidal thoughts, self-harm, stalking, and torture, while brief, they could be triggering for some people, so please make sure to take care of yourself. I strive to do the characters and the issues justice.

To being a boss bitch.

FINLEY, AGE 17

IF YOU'D ASKED me two years ago if I'd be handcuffed against a squad car, I would've first asked if you realized you were talking to me, the school nerd, and second, told you there wasn't any dimension where I, Miss Perfect, would be arrested.

Funny how trauma can change the whole trajectory of your life.

I might still be a nerd, but I was far from perfect—current circumstances solidified that fact.

"Do they really need to be so tight?" I huffed, pulling at them.

"You're lucky it was me, Finley. I know you think this is all fun and games, but kids get shot all the time for doing the stupid shit you do," Officer

Friendly sighed, heavy disappointment in his voice as he read me my rights.

And yes, that was his real name. I often wondered if he went into the profession just because of how it would sound, making him the perpetually good cop?

I'd known him for most of my life, his daughter being part of the same skating club as my brother and… Well, yeah, I didn't hang out at the skating club much anymore, and Officer Friendly liked to remind me of who I'd been back then. I think he was just tired of arresting me and having to see my parents be even more disappointed in me.

Me too, Officer Friendly, me too.

And yet, here I was, making another reckless decision in order to fill the ever-increasing void in my life. Though, shoplifting, changing grades, making fake IDs, and driving without a license were all minor compared to this.

In the past, I'd always been let off with a warning and a call to my parents to pick me up at the station. But not tonight.

Fudge, I'd messed up. Big time.

Sighing, I banged my head against the window, cursing Blackhawk under my breath. He was supposed to be here, but he and our other teammate, Obsidian, had never shown. I was beginning to think

I'd been setup. Shuffling in my red stilettos, I cursed my outfit of choice for the evening.

Double fudge, I was a gullible idiot. I *had* been setup. It was official. Finley Reyes was a loser. Blackhawk hadn't been interested. Just another guy to make me look like an idiot.

"I need to search you; spread your legs," the female officer said dryly.

Rolling my eyes, I sighed and did as she asked, spreading my legs. I tried not to think about the fact that this cop was getting further than any boy had before. Just another reminder of how much of a loser I was.

"Clean," she reported before opening the door. "Duck your head."

I had two seconds to process what she said before my head was pushed forward to get into the car. Climbing in, I tried not to flash the cops as I awkwardly flailed around with my hands behind me. Sitting sideways against the seat, I tried to figure a way out of this mess. When nothing came to mind, I dropped my head and noticed my red dress had risen up, reminding me how stupid I was. I looked more like a hooker than a spy.

Who wore a red cocktail dress with matching stilettos to steal something?

Me, that was who.

The girl who thought it might be her first actual date, but instead, apparently was a setup to take the fall. Not that I was entirely innocent, I'd gone into this mission knowing what I was doing. It was my last test before I was inducted into, The MidKnight Guild, the dark web club I'd stumbled upon a year ago.

Though, since I'd gotten caught, I probably hadn't passed. I'd just add it to the list of things I'd lost tonight.

My freedom—I was sure to be grounded until I was thirty by my parents after this stunt.

My friends—if you couldn't hack the initiation, you didn't belong.

My first crush—it was a pretty clear sign of rejection when the boy you liked let you get arrested.

I couldn't deny it any longer. I was an absolute mess, and now everyone would know it, too. It was hard to pretend you were okay, hiding behind white lies to everyone you knew, when your guilt would be splashed across the front page of tomorrow's paper.

I'd like to say I had my reasons, my best friend had disappeared, and no one seemed to care. But at this point, I'd done it for myself. Something about the rush of the job, cracking into a system you weren't supposed to be in, and taking what you wanted filled my veins with more emotion than I'd felt in years. And I craved it like an addict.

Sariah might've been the reason I started, but I kept going because I liked how it made me feel—alive. I just never meant for anyone to get hurt, myself included. It was dumb to think that no one would. I could see that now.

Obsidian and Blackhawk had been my blind spots. They made me feel like I belonged, and I hadn't felt that in years. If only it all hadn't gone so wrong. There was too much damage now, too many sins on my hands to just brush it all off.

No, I needed to make a stand, and that started with taking him down. No one made a fool of me and got to pretend like it hadn't happened. Blackhawk would rue the day he made me his enemy. We'd see who was laughing when it was all said and done.

Fire filled my veins, a scorching sense of righteousness accompanied by a need to mete out my own justice.

But as Officer Friendly listed all the charges they could bring against me, a sickening feeling developed in my stomach and I wondered who I even was anymore. I hadn't meant for any of this to happen. Where *had* it all gone so wrong?

As the lights flashed against the dark night on the

drive toward the police station, through my finger-prints being taken, and my mug shot, I tuned out all the thoughts and feelings and focused on one thing, and one thing only—revenge.

It would have to do for now.

PRESENT DAY, FINLEY, AGE 22

ASA'S FINGERS pumped inside me, filling me with pleasure, and I knew that we wouldn't stop this time. My hand gripped his cock, and I dragged my hand down, feeling how hard he was. Peering into his eyes, I saw the need reflected there, and I nodded, glad that we seemed to be on the same page. He reached over with his free hand, grabbing a condom, and I watched as he tore it open, sliding it on. It truly was a marvel to behold, and I was sad it might be the only time I got to see it.

Part of me hated what I was doing, but the other part of me, the one that had come to rule more often than not recently, relished in the dark ecstasy of our actions. It felt right that the first time we made love would be the day I was planning to leave.

"You sure? You're ready?" he asked, stopping at my entrance as he stared down at me.

"I'm ready. I want this." I pulled his face down, kissing him as I wrapped my legs around him. Asa braced his arms above me, stopping himself from entering me.

"I want to see your face," he said, pulling back, looking me deep in the eyes. Sucking in a breath, I nodded, staring back at him.

Slowly, oh, so slowly, he began to push in. Asa watched my every reaction, ready to stop this if it was too much. But I knew there was no way I was letting him stop.

It might seem weird that my boyfriend of almost eight months and I were just now having sex, but it wasn't from a lack of trying. At first, he'd wanted to hold off, making sure we really knew one another, and then there had been the kidnapping. But once we'd crossed every base multiple times, I was going insane.

The first time we tried was a disaster. Quickly followed by the second, third, and fourth. I wondered if I'd permanently scarred my boyfriend when he hadn't tried again for almost two months.

But here we were, attempt number I didn't even

remember, and I knew without a shadow of a doubt that it would work. It had to because I was out of time.

"You okay?" he asked, and I nodded, smoothing my hands over his hair.

"Yeah, I'm great. Don't stop."

Asa nodded, pushing in a little further, and I used my feet to push on his amazing buns of steel, propelling him even deeper into me. Once he was seated, we both let out a sigh of relief.

Peering down into my eyes, he brushed his thumb across my cheek. "Ready?" He smiled, a giddy excitement taking over. There wouldn't be any disruptions, family emergencies, illnesses, or broken beds to stop us this time. No, this morning, we would cross that line in our relationship, and then I would break his heart.

Bit morbid there, self.

Closing my eyes, I couldn't think about what I was doing this evening; I just wanted to focus on this moment between us now. It was selfish of me, but if Asa didn't forgive me, I wanted to have one experience of sex with him. As he began to pull out and push back in, I wondered if I just liked to punish myself.

Because losing this would be akin to torture.

"Fudge, you feel good," I heaved, my breath

coming out in a moan that even I was impressed by. Asa smiled his million-dollar smile, and butterflies erupted, my core tingling with need.

"I could say the same, but you sound so much cuter saying it."

Sticking out my tongue, I soon forgot my annoyance at him as he rolled back into me, his pelvic bone rubbing right against my clit. Arching my back, I pressed my boobs into him, the sensitive peaks brushing against his hard pecs. Moaning, my head fell back as I enjoyed the sensations.

"Yes, fuck, Finley, you feel more amazing than I even imagined. I knew this would be everything."

My perfect boyfriend leaned back, lifting my hips as he upped his pace, thrusting in and out of me quicker. I stared up at his perfect physique, getting wet at how hot he was. Blond hair, green eyes, and tanned muscles from hockey were all on display as he lost himself in me.

Picking me up by my ass, he brought our chests back together, kissing me with an intensity I hadn't felt from him yet. I never knew if Asa held himself back at times from politeness, fear, or worry. Either way, I was glad his wild side seemed to have taken over, allowing him to plunder me like the dick-loving-slut I was.

"More, more," I chanted, wanting him to fill me

up as much as possible. His fingers tightened on my hips, and I wrapped my legs tighter, the muscles in my thighs screaming as I clung to him. Weaving my fingers through his hair, I pulled as he brought me to my peak, my orgasm crashing over me. My muscles clenched, and I squeezed him as they began to pulse, screaming out my release.

"Yes!" I wheezed, my voice gone from the loud moan that had just released.

Asa grunted, slamming into me one more time as he slumped down on the bed, his cock twitching in me. We lay there for a while, our breathing returning to normal, before he rolled over and disposed of his condom. He turned back, and I grabbed his hand, needing to say something before losing my nerve.

"I love you, Asa."

He stopped, peering down at me, love shining in his eyes. "I love you, Fin." He dropped down, his lips catching mine as he gave me a kiss. When he pulled back, I had tears in my eyes, and he looked at me with concern.

"What is it, Fin? Do you regret it?"

Shaking my head, I grabbed his cheeks, wanting to touch him as much as possible. "No, no, that's not it. I'm just so happy."

"Then why do you look like you're saying the opposite?" he asked.

Sucking in a breath, I held it, trying to slow my heart. "I'm good. So, good. I promise. I just wanted you to know how I felt. You must remember this moment. That everything here was real. Promise me?"

"Why does it feel like you're trying to prepare me for something?" he asked, ignoring my question.

"I'm not. I just want to remember the good times."

"Well, there are many more to come, babe. Let's get dressed before my sister comes and tries to ruin our fun." Asa laughed, walking to the shower.

I watched his butt as he walked away, hoping that he would still think that when I did what I needed to do. Regardless, it was a risk I had to take.

THE WEIGHT of my decision sat heavily on my shoulders, leaving a bad taste in my mouth. Was I really going to do this? Could I? It felt so wrong to leave, but the more I thought about it, the more I realized I needed to. Picking up the pen, I wrote the hardest letter of my life.

Dear Asa,

Selfishly, I want you not to hate me, but since I

already hate myself for what I'm doing, it's unlikely you won't.

I have to go.

I have to right a wrong I made years ago and put that part of my past to bed. I thought I was over it, but if this past year has shown me anything, it's that trauma and bad decisions have a way of catching up to you.

The night I was taken reminded me of how reckless I can be and how I rely on the goodness of others to get me out of trouble. I can't be that girl anymore. I won't be that girl.

I want to feel strong when I look in the mirror, but all I see is a frightened girl who can't figure out what she wants.

Everything in my life is going well, and on paper, it's perfect. You're the best boyfriend a girl could ever have. My parents are finally listening to me and being honest. My brother is happy and skating again. My best friend is back and living her life free of the men who tried to control her. And yet, inside, I feel like I don't belong with any of you.

I'm not good, Asa.

There are so many things in my past that I regret, so many decisions I made in the pursuit of the truth, that now fill me with dread. One day, if you can forgive me, I'll tell you about them, I promise. I'm done hiding, and that starts with facing them and, well, *him*.

I hope you know I love you, Asa. And I pray that this will clear my head of all the misguided and confusing thoughts that seem to live up there. I want a life with you. I know I can be happy if I get rid of the darkness surrounding me. I need to purge my sins once and for all, which points back to the man who was the first to darken me.

I wish I could say how long it will be and when I'll be back. But the truth is, I can't. I don't know the answer to that. I just know that I need to do this now and to do that, I have to go off the grid.

I promise you this isn't about Milo or Cohen. I don't know what I feel for them, but that's something we can talk about when I get back if you want. I know I don't deserve any allowances made on my behalf for doing this, so if you forgive me and your decision is to not talk about them, then I'll accept it. I just wanted you to know this wasn't about them, and I'll stop ignoring the conversation we need to have around it. I promise.

I'm sorry to do this after the amazing morning we shared as well. Again, I was being selfish and knowing I wanted to experience it once with you in case I never got to again. I hope you understand.

I'm afraid no one else will, and Sawyer and my brother will try to come after me.

Please, I need to do this on my own. I promise to be safe, and I'll get back in contact when I can.

If this is the last time I get to speak with you, I just want you to know that you were the best thing to ever happen to me. I love you, Asa, and I hope to see you again.

Love, Fin

Wiping my tears, I laid down the pen and folded the paper into three, sliding it into the envelope. It was odd how such a heartbreaking letter could fit on a single sheet of paper. My whole world was about to shatter because of a few paragraphs.

A sound in the hallway had me hurrying in my task, and I slipped the letter into my journal, picked up my phone, and pretended to be scrolling social media just as someone entered my room.

"Fin, come on, it's time for dinner, and then we have to sing to Rhett. If we take too long, he'll escape, and we'll never be able to force him to sit with the party hat ever again," my best friend said, giving me a look.

Schooling my face, I nodded, pasting a smile on it. "Sure, one sec. I just need to send a text. I don't want Rhett to go all grumpy butt on us," I teased, hoping the mention of her sourpuss boyfriend would distract her.

"You're not wrong. You're okay, though, right? You've been distant, and I miss you." She walked into the room, giving me a concerned look.

"I'm great, promise." Standing, I took a few steps toward her as I pulled up my conversation with Milo, my last chance to back out at my fingertips.

ME: Everything is set.
Milo: I'll be there in an hour.
ME: See you then.

"Okay, let's go." I hooked my arm in hers, dragging her along so she wouldn't start to investigate more. Sawyer couldn't help it, she was a good best friend, but I didn't need her looking into anything too deeply if I wanted this to work.

And I *needed* this to work.

Two

FINLEY

EVERYONE LAUGHED and celebrated as Rhett blew out his candles. The big grump had a smile on his face despite wearing a paper hat, and I knew I'd never seen him happier than here at his Granny's house that he'd inherited. The house was magnificent, and the ocean was literally right outside the back door. It was paradise.

So why did I feel like crying? It only reminded me how happy I should've been but wasn't. All I could think about was how miserable I was, cementing my decision to leave. It was now or never. I couldn't keep living a half-life where I pretended to be "perfect Fin" any longer.

Asa placed his arm around me, knocking me out of my thoughts as he drew me close, and I forced a smile. He was what real happiness looked like. I only wished I could feel as happy as he did. He'd been the absolute best after I'd been kidnapped by the Council. He'd been caring, patient, and understanding of my mood swings. I knew my silence was hard on him, yet he'd given me time to figure it out at my pace. The worst part was I wished he hadn't been so nice about it because then I wouldn't feel as guilty for pushing him away.

But I'd fallen in love with him for a reason, and now I was punishing him for his eternal sunshine. It wasn't fair, and I knew it. He deserved better from me. Except now, I was going to ask him not to hate me for leaving.

It might sound irrational, but I couldn't get past the trauma. I hated that I flinched every time someone knocked on the door or came in with a "you'll never believe this?" I hated that I constantly thought about boys I shouldn't. The guilt had built to an oppressive weight, and I was suffocating. Every day, I walked along a perpetual ledge, constantly re-balancing as I waited for the other shoe to drop, knowing it was just around the corner. Because it was always around the corner.

Funny how shoes were what had gotten me into this mess in the first place.

Asa handed me a plate, and I pasted on a smile. I

looked around at our friends and family gathered, trying to soak in their happiness like a leech.

My best friend, Asa's twin sister, was surrounded by her seven boyfriends, one of which was my brother, Henry. They stared back at her with love in their eyes, and despite everything they'd gone through last fall with the Council, they were all stronger than ever. If anything, it had brought them all closer.

I couldn't say the same for myself. I'd been kidnapped, drugged, and put up for auction by the Council due to my own stupid mistakes. Sleep evaded me, and nightmares of the past and present played on an unrelenting loop, adding to my constant state of awareness. My secrets were catching up with me, and I couldn't hold them off any longer.

How Asa was still with me, I didn't know. How anyone had put up with my sour moods and distance only proved how much better they all were than me. They'd all rallied, but I was failing miserably. Once again.

The simple truth was, I didn't belong.

Not with the things I'd done. Not with my past. I hated that the sins of my youth were now destroying my future. It turned out that burying things wasn't a healthy way to cope. Shoving some cake into my mouth, I knew what I needed to do. It only confirmed that my decision was right.

I couldn't stay.

This trip had been the last push I needed to convince myself things had to change. In order to live the life I wanted, to feel happy… I had to make right the damage I created when I was seventeen.

I had to face *him*.

The only thing standing in my way was me, and it was time I faced the mistakes of my past instead of running.

Except now, I had to run.

I needed to distance myself from the people I loved—especially Asa. He was too good, too pure, and I couldn't taint him with the sins of a misguided youth. No, this couldn't come back on him. I didn't think we'd survive it, and losing him that way would crush me.

It was better for me to go now. This way, I could control the fallout, and perhaps once I was done, once I'd completed my mission, we could start again. Better. Stronger.

It was the only sliver of hope I'd allow myself to hang on to.

"Want to go with everyone to the beach? I think some sea turtles were laying their eggs?" Asa asked, bringing me back to the present.

I looked down, realizing I'd eaten all my cake and hadn't even noticed. Turning into him, I kissed his cheek as I tried to hide the falling tear.

"I've got a headache. I'll call it a night, but you should go."

Asa observed me, trying to gauge my feelings. He'd done that a lot in the past six months. "I can stay with you."

He took my hand, squeezing it. The comfort he was providing was too much, and I knew I was about to cave. Shaking my head, I cupped his cheek, taking in his face for one last time. I wanted to remember this look of love he had in case he never held it again.

"No, it's okay. I promise I'm fine. Go, have fun and make sure none of them get into trouble. I don't think anyone can deal with seeing Sawyer naked again." I chuckled, trying to distract him from my goodbye.

Asa grimaced, recalling how we'd been greeted yesterday morning before responding. "Are you sure? I don't mind staying back."

"Positive. I know how much you were hoping to see the turtles. Go. I promise, I'm good." He hesitated and I could see him wavering. Buckling down, I spread my most perfect Fin smile across my face. Asa melted, giving in.

"Okay. I'll check on you in a bit then."

"I love you, Asa," I said, holding the tears from my voice.

He kissed my cheek. "I love you, Fin."

It was everything I needed to hear and what I would hold on to over the next few months. He walked off, joining the group, and I waved, trying to keep in my emotions, not wanting them to see what I was feeling. I needed this time to make my escape.

Once they were all gone, my body relaxed for a second before the adrenaline of what was to come surged through me. My heart began to race as I walked up the stairs to my room. This was it. I was really doing it.

Stepping into the space, I could smell Asa's cologne mixed with my perfume, and I took a breath, needing to store the memory. Wiping the tears that fell unashamedly now, I pulled the letter I'd written earlier out of my journal, and placed it on his pillow. Tears dropped onto it as I tried to wipe them away. It was cowardly to leave this way, but I wouldn't have the courage to do it any other way. I just prayed he'd forgive me.

Changing quickly, I grabbed the bag I'd packed with the essentials and a couple of outfits and tiptoed down the stairs to the front door in case anyone had returned. Tears trailed down my face quicker as I left everything and everyone I knew behind. I opened the thick front door and walked through with determination, promising myself it was worth it.

Dressed in black leather pants, a black top, and black boots, I blended into the night as I crept down the driveway. I might be running away, but I could still do it in style. No one would ever accuse me of being boring at least.

I spotted the car idling for me at the end of the road. A warm sensation filled my body at Milo coming through, but I shoved it away with everything else I refused to look at where he was concerned.

I knew leaving this way would hurt; it was a punch to the gut, but I'd run out of options. If I didn't do this, if I didn't go now, I'd always be watching over my shoulder, waiting for him, never truly growing. Regret would rule my life, and I didn't want to live that way anymore.

I would never be happy—not until he'd been dealt with.

Shoving my bag into the tiny trunk of the expensive sports car, I opened the door, sliding in.

Milo smiled over at me, his eyes twinkling in the lights of the interior. "You get out, okay?"

"Yeah. No one saw me. Thanks," I paused, swallowing, "for doing this for me."

"You know I'm here for you, Finley, whatever you

need. Besides, it's kind of my thing to be the one to save you."

Smiling, I tried to ignore the confused butterflies erupting at his words. It didn't matter, though. They were there, swirling around with everything else I felt guilty about. I was tired of feeling guilty. Buckling up, I settled in for the drive and pulled out the list I'd made.

1. Find him
2. Take him down
3. Make him pay

At one time, Blackhawk had been my salvation until he became my damnation. It was time I became my own saving grace.

My sins were dark, my spirit broken, but I was no longer weak. It was time I remembered who I'd been. It was time I returned to Oblivion.

And this time, my stilettos wouldn't just be sinful. No, this time, they would be deadly.

MOST OF THE ride was quiet as I pondered over my choices. While I knew I needed to do it, I couldn't deny the pit in my stomach that I was making the wrong choice. I was risking everything and hoping the people in my life loved me enough to forgive me after it was all said and done.

"You hungry?" Milo asked, and I turned, blushing. I'd kind of forgotten he was there. Not that I thought the car was driving itself, but I'd zoned out so far that I felt alone in time and space.

"No, I ate before…" I didn't need to say anything else. He nodded, keeping his eyes on the road.

"You know, we haven't talked much about what this is all about, just that you needed to escape for a while where no one could find you. Are you in trouble?"

"No." I shook my head, watching the trees fly by through the car window. "I'm trying to rectify a mistake."

"Is it going to be dangerous?" he asked, his voice sounding odd, so I faced him.

"It could be. Why?"

I watched as his hands gripped the wheel harder, his jaw flexing a little, and I couldn't figure out why he was so upset about this.

"You seem, I don't know, more upset than I thought you'd be."

He laughed in a way that let me know he didn't find it funny. "Oh? Is that so?" Milo shook his head, making me even more unsure of what was going on with him. I kept watching, hoping if I stared at him long enough, he'd cave and give in to the pressure.

A few minutes went by, and he sighed, glancing over at me. He put on his blinker, the sound filling the space as he turned down another dark street.

"It's nothing. Forget I said anything."

I frowned, my brow creasing in concern. "I feel like I just failed a test I didn't know I was taking."

He chuckled again, this one sounding a little more like himself, the carefree guy I'd met in one of the darker moments of my life.

"You don't even see how amazing you are, Fin. That's all. I worry about you. I... *care* about you. More than I should since you have a boyfriend, but the simple fact is, I do. But that's not your problem."

"I..." I swallowed, not sure how to respond. "Thank you, Milo. I couldn't have done any of this without you. I'm just not in the place to really make any big decisions. I need to do this before I can even think about what my life will look like after."

"You keep saying that, but I wonder if it's more an excuse than a real reason."

I shook my head, the rebuttal quick on my tongue to argue, but it died when I looked at his face, at the pain I seemed to be causing him. Regardless of the reason, I knew I had to focus on the future, which meant fixing the past.

"It's all I can offer you," I finally said, turning back in my seat and sliding down into it. I laid my head back against the plush leather and closed my eyes, pretending I was going to sleep. It was shitty of me and cowardly, but after the emotional toll of leaving, I was spent, and it was all I had left.

Besides, I was great at ignoring things until they blew up in my face.

A FEW HOURS LATER, we pulled up to a hotel, and I sat up, stretching, going along with my fake sleep ruse. Milo chuckled at me, and I knew he hadn't bought it but was at least indulging me in my delusion.

"Sit tight. I'll go get the room. I know you want to stay off cameras."

Nodding, I smiled my thanks, reaching across to squeeze his hand. "Thank you, Milo. I know I've been a crappy friend, but I appreciate everything you've done for me."

His lip curled up on one side, and he squeezed my hand. It hurt my heart a little to see him so unsure of things, especially when I was the cause.

Sighing, I sat back and pulled out a burner phone to check in on the situation back at the house. I knew

I had only a small opportunity before they got Cohen or someone else techy on the job, and then I would lose my window, but for now, I would be selfish and peer into their world to see the mayhem I had caused. A part of me felt I deserved to witness the pain I'd inflicted on them.

Clicking on the camera icon, I cloaked my location and then selected the main room. I'd been busy hacking into the security system yesterday while everyone was swimming in the pool. The camera pulled up easily, and I found the room filled with a few people talking.

I hesitated, debating if I wanted to hear what they were saying or not. I might not like what I heard, and it wouldn't be something I could un-hear from my friends once it was out there. But again, I was a glutton for punishment and felt I deserved whatever vitriol they wanted to throw at me.

"How far do you think she's made it?" Sawyer asked, pacing back and forth.

"Maybe we should just let her do what she needs to?" Mateo offered.

"It could be dangerous. She's doing her usual 'I can fix it on my own' thing, and that never ends well," my brother said, sighing into his hands as he rubbed his face. "Why now?"

I'd been avoiding looking at Asa, but when he

spoke up, I could no longer ignore the forlorn expression he wore or the dejected way his body melded into the sofa.

"Because whatever it is, it's more important than us," he said, throwing the letter I'd written onto the table and standing up. "I'm sorry Sis, but I can't stay here. I'm going to stop by a few places I like to surf and spend some time on my own. You won't be mad if I miss the rest of the vacation?"

My best friend stood, walking over to Asa, and wrapped her arms around her twin. Despite the fact they'd only known about each other for less than a year, they had already developed a tight bond.

"I'll miss you, but I understand. Let me know when you make it somewhere, and make sure to keep me updated. I don't want you to run off and do anything foolish because you're heartbroken."

He kissed her head, a tear falling down my face at the misery I was causing. This wasn't helping, but I couldn't find it in myself to turn it off now that I was watching.

Rhett stormed into the room, a phone in his hand. "I got a hold of your father, baby. Samson will have Cohen look into some possible leads and brief us back in Utah. We'll find her, and then I'll wring her neck for skipping out on us like this."

He pulled his tiny girlfriend into his arms, and I

realized I'd had enough; plus, I didn't really need to see any mushy stuff between one of my good friends and my bestie. There were some lines I wanted to keep. I was already scarred enough from walking in on a naked scene between her and my brother that I could've lived my whole life without.

Closing out the app, I laid my head back, debating with myself again. "They'll be okay. They'll forgive you. You had to do this. It's okay to pick yourself every once and a while."

"Talking to yourself?" Milo asked, and I jumped, not realizing the door had opened.

"Oh, did you hear that?" My face flushed, and I unhooked my seatbelt to get out of the door he held open for me. He smirked, not answering, which was an answer in and of itself. He handed me my bag, and I pulled out a hoodie, pulling it over my head to hide my face, and we walked into the back entrance together, his frame blocking mine.

"I'll get a few hours of sleep before hitting the road. The car I got for you will be dropped off in the morning, and I told the guy to drop it and the other items you asked for at the front desk and for them to slide the envelope under the door. You should have minimal contact here, helping to hide your presence as long as you need. I even have the room for a week if you change your mind."

His hand was on the lower part of my back as we walked, and I tried not to focus on how nice his heat felt. "Thank you, Milo. Once again, I don't know how I'll ever repay you."

Milo dropped his hand, using the key card to open the door and pushing it open into a luxurious room. "In my life, friendship is something I value more than anything. But," he paused, biting his lip as he debated, "maybe we could go to dinner sometime?"

He adjusted his glasses as I watched him, and I fought with myself. I knew how I wanted to answer, but I was back to whether I deserved it or not. Someone as reprehensible as me shouldn't deserve such a nice guy like Milo to like her.

"I'm not sure I'm worth that much, but if it's what you want, then I will."

"You make yourself sound like the world's worst criminal, Fin." He rolled his eyes, moving further into the room. "Don't forget who my family is."

I nodded, setting my bag on the bed closest to the door. While I knew what he meant, considering his family was part of a secret organization bent on taking over the world, it wasn't the same. At least, not in my eyes. I'd chosen to do the things I'd done; he just had the unfortunate luck to be born into the Council.

The Council was made up of seven families that used the Olympics and the young athletes training for them as their mules to import and export everything from drugs, weapons, and stolen artifacts, while also holding the market in every major industry. Despite the Council being taken down last winter, he still had connections. Milo's family had been on the automotive side of things, which helped me out when I needed a car my family couldn't trace.

While Milo was a Bellamy, he wasn't part of their misdeeds, making him innocent, in my opinion. He'd even saved me from being auctioned off in one of their human trafficking rings. It was the first night we met and the night I realized I liked him as more than a friend. There was just that pesky detail about my boyfriend. And while my bestie Sawyer had found a way to have seven men adore her, I didn't feel I was that lucky, or perhaps, worthy enough to be greedy.

Though, even as I thought that, I knew Sawyer wasn't being greedy. She loved her men, and they loved her. It was just how it was.

But yet, the logic didn't seem to fit me. I was too selfish, too undeserving, and too reckless to have more than I was allowed.

"Do you need the restroom?" I asked, fidgeting

on the spot. Everything felt too much at the moment with us in this room alone.

"No, I'm just going to sleep."

Biting my lip, I felt like I was letting him down and that I should say something, but for once, words were failing me.

"Okay, well, um, thanks again." I picked up my bag and walked into the bathroom, leaning against the door as it closed. I didn't really need anything in here, but it felt like the safest space for the time being. Stripping off all my clothes, I took a long shower, hoping it would provide enough time for him to fall asleep and allow me to continue to avoid the conversation I needed to have.

"Yeah, because that keeps working out for you," I berated, hissing at myself under the water.

Sucking it up, I got out, brushed my hair and teeth, and applied the world's most generous amount of lotion one could ever use.

"You're just stalling. And talking to yourself. You're losing it, Fin."

Rolling my eyes, I threw everything into my bag and braced myself. When I stepped out into the room, one lamp was on, cascading the room into shadows. Quietly, I tiptoed over to the bed and crawled under the covers, lying on the pillow.

It took a while, but eventually, I quieted my mind

enough that I could fall asleep. It felt like only a few seconds later when a hand brushed the hair out of my face as a body hovered over me. I knew it was Milo. He was the only person I knew who smelled like rainfall and a campfire. His scent surrounded me, and I fought everything in me not to open my eyes and give in to the yearning I knew I'd find staring at me.

As I kept my breathing even, he bent down and kissed my forehead softly. "Be safe, darling." His fingers trailed over my cheek, and I urged my body not to give in to the shudder it wanted to do. When the door clicked shut a few seconds later, I braved it and opened my eyes, finding the room empty, the sun starting to rise.

The absolute silence weighed on me, and once again, I wondered if I was doing the right thing. An overwhelming sense of fear, dread, and loneliness filled me, and I replayed the last few seconds with Milo in my head. I could no longer stop the tears from falling. The night everything changed no longer wished to be buried and it rose up, reminding me how stupid I was.

THAT NIGHT

Oblivion: Do we all know our parts?

Blackhawk: Yes, little hacker, we've been over it a few times. We're good. We got this, babe.

Whenever he called me that, my pulse raced, and I wished I could hear him saying it. Tonight would be the first time we met in person, and I was excited about putting a face to the name, to the boy I'd been crushing on for a year.

Obsidian: After tonight, we'll be full members of MKG. Assuming we don't fuck up. I know I won't, so it's on you two.
Oblivion: Don't get your panties in a knot, Sid. We got this. I can hack circles around this system, and you know there hasn't been a lock I haven't been able to get through. We've been building up to this for a year. Trust your team.
Blackhawk: The only one who wears panties is you, Oblivion. Just to be sure, we should show each other.
Obsidian: Stop being a perv. You're right. We're the best.
Oblivion: Sure, you go first.
Obsidian: Don't let him devalue you. You're too good for that, Oblivion. He's just a pretty boy who happens to be good at coding.

Blackhawk: Ah, thanks for the compliment, Sid. I wish I could say the same for your face.

Obsidian: Bite me.

Blackhawk: Oh, fiesty. Now, go and review your program. It's important.

Obsidian: You're not the boss. If anyone is, it's me. I'm the oldest and have the most experience. You just want to flirt.

Blackhawk: Whatever you need to believe.

Oblivion: You two are cattier than the girls at school.

Obsidian: You should let me show them not to mess with geeks. I'd make them wish they never met you.

Oblivion: Maybe next week. I just want to focus on the mission.

Blackhawk: And they say romance is dead. Now, who's flirty?

Obsidian: Whatever. I gotta go. See you both in a few hours.

Obsidian signed off.

Blackhawk started a private chat.

Blackhawk: Ah, I hurt his feelings.

Oblivion: Yeah, I think you did. It's so unfair

you two know each other. I feel like the third wheel. Especially since Mongoose.

Blackhawk: Yeah, well, we won't talk about Mongoose. But you could never be the third wheel, little hacker.

Oblivion: Are you, you know, being flirty?

Blackhawk: Do you not know when a guy is hitting on you, little hacker?

Oblivion: Not really. Remember, I've never had a guy flirt with me? Most of them ignore me.

Blackhawk: I forget most of the time you're still in high school. Which reminds me… when do you turn 18 again?

Oblivion: In a few months. Why?

Blackhawk: No reason, jailbait.

Oblivion: You're only, what four years older than me? You act like it's a decade.

Blackhawk: Um, sure. Let's leave it at that.

Oblivion: You're infuriating.

Blackhawk: Are you nervous about our final mission? The other things were easier.

Oblivion: Maybe for you, but remember, I haven't been doing this as long. I only started a few years ago. It's all been hard for me.

Blackhawk: You're crazy talented for only doing it a few years, babe. Have you found any new information about your friend? Did my contact work out?

Oblivion: He's looking, but I'm starting to wonder if I'm crazy. I just can't accept that she's dead. I'd know it.

Blackhawk: She must be pretty special. I've never had a friend like that.

Oblivion: Not even Obsidian?

Blackhawk: We're roommates and only because we didn't know anyone else, not because we genuinely like each other.

Oblivion: I'm not sure if he'd say the same thing, but, well, you're my friend.

Blackhawk: God, I do love your innocence. Okay, I'll be your friend. I'll try not to corrupt you too much.

Oblivion: Too late for that.

Blackhawk: Look at you, being all flirty. I'm looking forward to meeting you tonight, little hacker. I'll see you soon.

Oblivion: See you soon.

Shutting the laptop, I set it aside as I kicked my legs up on the bed in happiness. The immediate need to tell Sariah arose, squelching a little of my joy. I wish I could tell her these things. I wish she was still here. I needed to find her. Henry was becoming a shell of the person he was. He hadn't been able to find another pairs skater, so he'd started speed skating. He'd become so withdrawn, though, I worried I would lose my brother, too.

I didn't know if I'd survive that. I couldn't lose him and Sariah. It was why tonight was so important. If I made it into the MKG, I'd have better connections and resources to dig deeper and find the information on where she went. It all hinged on tonight going well.

Not only would I finally belong somewhere and be able to uncover the secret of Sariah's disappearance—I refused to say death—I would finally get to meet the first boy I'd managed to semi-flirt with.

Deciding to go for it, I pulled out the ruby red dress and matching heels. When the stilettos arrived, I knew they were from him. We'd all talked about our weaknesses, and I'd said mine were shoes. A few days later, the most gorgeous pair of red stilettos arrived.

Coincidence? No, I didn't believe in coincidences.

The note had just said, *"I can't wait to see you in them,"* letting me know even more that tonight was the night I should wear them—the night we'd meet and our futures would change forever.

Once I was dressed, I climbed out my window, holding the shoes in my hand as I climbed over the overhang and slipped to the ground. Placing them on, I quickly made my way to Sullivan Street behind my house, where I'd told the car to meet me. The sedan waited at the curb, and I quickly hurried over, sliding in.

It wasn't until later, when I was being handcuffed, that the implications of the night had set in. I was dumb, naive, and now a juvenile delinquent. Go me.

PRESENT DAY

The burner phone pinged, drawing me back to the present. Sucking back my tears, I dried my eyes and climbed out of bed. Crying wouldn't do any good. I couldn't let myself go down that hole again. I had to focus on the mission. The memory had reminded me just how important it was.

When I pulled out my phone and signed into the app the notification had come from, it made my last thoughts even more detrimental.

Blackhawk: Oblivion, babe, where have you been? I've missed you.

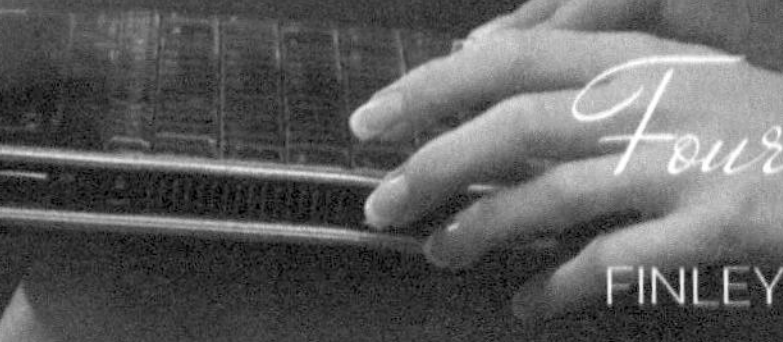

Four

FINLEY

I STARED at the message like it was alive and he was about to jump off the tiny screen and strangle me where I sat. A million emotions coursed through me at the thought as fear took hold. I thought I was ready, that the moment I stepped away from every- thing else and faced this, it would all come to a head, and I'd know what to do.

But as I stared at the message, sweat building on my upper lip, I realized I had absolutely no freaking clue what I was doing.

Outside of my 'get revenge' list, it seemed I was poorly equipped to actually do anything else. Which in the grand scheme of things didn't surprise me. It was my fatal flaw, after all. This time it seemed, I'd been the recipient of my own assumptions.

Not begrudging my brother his talent because I knew he had his own battles to fight, but growing up in his shadow had been hard. Henry was the one who seemed to flawlessly get everything right the first time. When he and Sariah started to win competitions, the spotlight around them became even brighter.

As theirs increased, it felt like all the light around me was sucked away into a vacuum, and I was left with a mere glimmer. I didn't like feeling envious of my best friend and brother, so I found ways to share in their light, persuading others I had something worth looking at.

That was the start of my downfall.

I faked so many things, I convinced even myself I could do them, forgetting half the time I was only pretending.

But when I got a taste of that limelight, I couldn't let it go, wanting it more and more like an addict. Once people thought you were perfect, it was hard to be anything other than that.

But it was exhausting constantly pretending, and when Sariah went missing, I no longer had their light to steal.

It was a sad realization that you missed your best friend because she made you brighter.

Standing, I walked over to the window, peeking behind the curtains to stare out into the parking lot. The sun was starting to rise, the day beginning, and I felt none of it. A sinking weight settled on me, and I struggled to stand as it pressed into me. Bit by bit, it would break me down, crushing me until I was nothing but a pile of rubble.

Squeezing my eyes shut, I pressed my fists into them, begging the pressure to lessen. All the thoughts swirled, folding into themselves, and I was on the verge of losing it.

"Shit, shit, shit."

I hadn't felt this out of control since... *No! Don't go there.*

The memory I worked so hard to control came roaring back now that I was alone, filling all my crevices with the darkness, sucking out all the joy, and finding any space to root itself as I fell back into a flashback of how I ended up on the path that would lead to my greatest sin.

FINLEY, 16

Slamming the door, I stomped over to my desk, breathing heavily as I panted in and out.

"I hate you!" I yelled.

Dropping into the chair, the tears fell before my

butt even hit the seat. Pulling my legs up, I wrapped my arms around them, leaning my head against my knees as I sobbed, rocking slightly.

No one understood. No one seemed to care. I was so alone in this house. I missed my friend.

The thoughts repeated as I continued to sit there, stewing in my feelings, wondering if I would ever find happiness again. Maybe it was time to just say fuck it all and do everyone a favor? If I was gone, they wouldn't have to worry or deal with me anymore.

Sliding open the top drawer, I placed one knee on the ground, staring into the dark space. It resembled my mind so much that it felt both familiar and disarming. I was so tired of feeling this way. I could just take care of it.

Pulling out the bottle of pills I'd stolen, I spun them around, the contents clicking against one another as I twirled them. I'd done it slowly, taking a pill here and there from my mother, grandparents, and even friends' houses I visited.

It was like an odd fixation I had now to open people's medicine cabinets and see what they left out for everyone to see. I didn't even know what some of them were, but I had to assume that this much of anything wouldn't be good for a person to ingest.

Blue pills, yellow ones, red ones, and even some

white tablets filled the old container. Some days, I'd pull it out, twirling it around like this, and the knowledge I had a way out was enough to calm me.

Other times, I'd dump them out onto my desk, sorting them by color and counting, taking myself a little bit closer to the edge before I tossed them back in, the anxiety gone, and my breathing returned to regular.

Today, it felt like nothing short of going through with it would help.

Twisting the cap, I poured them into my hand, feeling their weight as I jostled them around. It always shocked me how something so insignificant as these small things could create such chaos in one's body. The sweet oblivion they would provide, the quietness of my thoughts for once, felt worth any chaos I might endure.

Grabbing the water bottle out of my bookbag, I stared down at the colorful handful. This was it. It was now or never. Lifting my hand closer, I watched them move in slow motion like I was witnessing it outside of myself. As I reached my mouth, I opened it, ready to dump them all in and finally say goodbye to all this self-hatred, turmoil, and disgust I felt inside.

My hand froze, and I stared, and stared, and stared.

A ping from my computer jolted me, and I tensed, almost falling out of my chair. My hand closed over the pills, only a few escaping. Quickly, I dumped the ones I had clasped between my palm into the bottle and jumped down to collect the few that had fallen. It felt vital to have them all. If I was missing even one, I wouldn't be able to go through with it.

I tried to ignore that by placing parameters on my own suicide, that might mean I wasn't actually ready to take that step. But it felt too much like failing at something else to say it out loud.

The computer pinged again as I reached under my desk, reaching for one blue pill that had bounced all the way to the back. Grunting, I pressed against the wood, straining to reach it. The particle board cut into my arm, scraping it, but I pushed on. I ignored how much effort I was putting into keeping the thing I was banking on killing me like it was my lifeline.

Finally, my fingers clasped around the pill, and I drew it back, my heart returning to normal as I placed it into the bottle. *There, everything was right again.* Screwing on the cap, I tucked it safely back into my drawer. I needed it close to remind myself it was there. It had become a weird safety blanket.

The ping sounded a third time, and I turned to my computer, opening the message that kept going off. It was a person I'd met on a random site responding to my request. Adrenaline began to rush through me at what this could mean.

> **User584:** I think I found what you were looking for. I'll send you the invite. The password is l3mon_fizz!e.
> **User827:** Sweet! You're the absolute best.

I tapped my fingers on my desk as I anxiously waited for the message to come through. I'd been teaching myself coding for the past year and had taken a few classes at the local college. It had been the one thing my parents had let me do, thinking it would help to distract me. I didn't tell them it was to help me find more information on Sariah. They could believe what they wanted.

The link popped up, and I hovered the mouse over it, a last-second urge to stop myself clawing at my mind. Glancing over at the picture frame on my desk, I took in the picture of the three of us, so young, carefree, and happy. When I looked at my brother now, he was a shell of himself. I couldn't stop until I had real answers.

Straightening my spine, I looked back at the monitor and clicked on the link, determination coursing through me.

The screen began to pixelate and went black, and I gulped, hoping I hadn't just been played until a command popped up.

C:/what is your code name?

The blinking cursor mocked me as it waited for me to enter my name. A hacker name, I needed a hacker name. Hmm, what could I be?

Fashionista? Too girly.

Little sister? Too dumb.

Dark Cloud? Too morbid.

For some reason, I pulled open the drawer, staring at the bottle of pills that had become the answer to my problems, hoping I'd find something within it. Though, the only solution they truly offered me was oblivion and a release from my darkness. The realization slammed into me, and I knew what my hacker name would be. It was really the only thing that made sense.

C:/Oblivion.

C:/Welcome to the dark web, Oblivion.

Password?

C:/l3mon_fizz!e

C:/ Access granted. You've been entered into

the pool for admittance to The MidKnight Guild. You'll be given a series of tasks to perform with fellow initiates. Fail to perform them, and you don't belong. Your success is in your hands. Do you accept?

C:/ Yes. I accept.

C:/Welcome to the games. We'll be in touch.

The screen returned to normal, and I exhaled, realizing I'd been holding my breath through the exchange. I was in!

Happiness and excitement, a foreign feeling, whirled to life in me, and I sat back, smiling. The drawer stood open, almost mocking me, reminding me what I'd been ready to do ten minutes earlier. Slamming it shut, I wasn't prepared to let it go yet, but I didn't need to necessarily be reminded of my weakness either.

Walking to my bed, I pulled another picture frame of my best friend and me off the nightstand, and I held it to my chest as I lay in bed.

"I'll find you, Sariah. I promise."

IN THE END, I did find her, but not because of the dark web. No, that had only led to my destruction.

I STAYED in the hotel room for a few days, licking my imaginary wounds. I was embarrassed to admit it took me that long to pull myself out of my funk, shower, and have a stern talking with myself. If I kept letting myself fall back into the past, I wouldn't be able to correct my future; I'd only be ruining it more.

"Time to suck it up, girl. Message him back and tell him how you really feel."

Taking a deep breath, I pulled out my most prized possession after my sewing machine—my custom-built laptop. Smoothing my hands over the surface, I touched the stickers I'd placed on it adoringly, reminding myself of what I'd intended when I'd settled on each of them. The one that caught my eye today was, "Nevertheless, she persisted." With one final push, I opened the lid and powered it on.

I used to get a jolt of adrenaline each time I sat in front of this screen, the thrill of a new adventure awaiting me on the other side. After the fallout with Blackhawk and Obsidian, it all felt too broken and contaminated. It took me a while to find I could use my skills for good, and my white hacking site was born.

"Though, how well did that turn out last time?" my sins whispered to me, reminding me how well I'd assisted someone who ended up being human trafficked anyway despite my 'help.'

Pushing that reminder to the far recesses of my mind, I knew I couldn't open that can of worms just yet. There were so many things attached to it, and I wasn't ready. I didn't know if I ever would be. It was much better to focus on the thing I could right now and strangle this demon instead of letting them all breed. Yeah, sound advice.

Signing into the app I hadn't frequented in years, I clicked on the message that had sent me spiraling.

Blackhawk: Oblivion, babe, where have you been? I've missed you.

There he was. It felt surreal that he was right there. My nightmare had been at my fingertips all along. Tapping my nails on the keyboard, I debated how to respond. I honestly thought he'd put up more of a fight. I hadn't expected to find him this soon. Now that I had, what did I say?

Hey, asshole, thanks for ruining my life. Now, please meet me at the 7-Eleven so I can kick you in the nuts?

No, I didn't think that would work. Plus, I wanted

to destroy him more than just leaving him unable to bear children. An idea formed, and I knew what I needed to do—exactly what they'd done to me.

Lure him into a false sense of security. Make him think we were friends and then crush his spirit. All the while, in the background, I'd destroy everything he loved and cherished. Nothing would be safe.

Unless he had a dog, then I'd just steal it and make him think it ran away. Yes, this was the way to go about it.

Feeling invigorated with my new plan, I cracked my knuckles and rested my fingers on the familiar keys. The power that lay beneath my fingertips was what always amazed me, pushing me to press them. If people only knew the real power they had to destroy others. Scratch that. I didn't need to go full rebellion, just revenge. And maybe some redemption for the other things.

Okay, now that I had my mindset, I typed in a response. Time to play a little game, asshole.

Oblivion: That's rich coming from you. I'm surprised your balls haven't shriveled up inside you from how much of a coward you are.

I hit send before I could take it back and realized I'd gone a little harsh, but it was fine, totally fine.

Crap! Crap! Crap! How did I unsend something? Fudge, why did I let myself think I could do this?

While I was having a mini panic attack, I missed the fact that he sent back a message. So when the ping sounded, I jumped, hitting a bunch of random keys. Furiously hitting delete, I forced my eyes up to read his reply.

Blackhawk: How I've missed your wit, little hacker. It's been lonely on here these past four years. But I must ask, why do you think I'm a coward?

I didn't even have to think anymore as I typed out my response. If he was here to chat, it was time to find out some information. The problem with finding Blackhawk all those years ago was that I didn't know much about his real identity outside of his hacker name and random facts we shared. I needed more than his favorite pizza this time if I was going to destroy him.

Oblivion: You're even more of one if you have to ask.

Oblivion: What have you been getting your-self into? It has been a while, hasn't it?

Okay, good, that was good. Ease him in nice and slow there. I waited, but nothing came, and eventually, I got bored, so I clicked on the next screen, my mouse hovering over the confirm button.

Did I want to violate my friends' privacy more? It wasn't so much I wanted to violate them, but the need to know how they were doing was thumping at my brain, desperate to know. At this point, the pain reminded me I was still vital, important to them. It was selfish to use their suffering to validate my own need to feel important, but it was what it was, and I couldn't stop myself now.

Besides, I was too much of a chicken to actually look at the one person I wanted to know the most about—Asa. Instead, I would vicariously feed off the others like a parasite, hoping to glean some knowledge to whet my curiosity.

Pushing the button, I didn't find anyone in the living room or the boardroom, so I clicked on the kitchen, hoping I'd find someone. I'd only put them in a few areas, not wanting to accidentally stumble across something I didn't want to see. Not that these areas were completely safe, so I shut my eyes, listening first before I peeked out.

When I only heard voices talking, I was glad to find they were clothed. Sawyer and my brother sat on the stools at the island, talking with Samson, Sawyer's dad.

"How could she just disappear with no trail?" Sawyer asked, hurt laced in her voice. "There's really nothing?"

"As of now, no. She covered her tracks well enough that we haven't been able to pick up any leads on what direction she was headed. We see her walk down the driveway, but once she's at a certain distance, it's like she just vanished. We've checked all the traffic cams and hotels within 100 miles and are still coming up short. We have to sit tight and wait for her to make a move."

"I think we should just let her be," my brother said, finally looking up. He had dark circles under his eyes, and I hated how much I seemed to be stressing him out.

"How can you say that?" Sawyer asked, gasping.

"Fin has been struggling for a while. She apparently needs to do this. Until then, she's not going to let herself be found. Not by us, at least. If we keep searching for her, we're only going to push her further underground, and then she might never return. At least this way, she has the chance to do what she needs without worrying we're going to send in the calvary."

"No. I disagree," Sawyer said, shaking her head. "I can't let her go off on her own. She's my best friend. I need to know she's safe."

My brother picked up her hand, smoothing his thumb over the top. "I know, Smalls. But you didn't see her after you were gone. She went to some dark places, did some things she regrets. I don't know everything that happened, but I do know I don't want my sister to feel she has to push everyone away forever. So, I'll give her some time to figure things out. I promise, I'm not letting her just ride off and fight her battles alone. I refuse to lose my sister, but for now, we let her. We need to focus on training and our competition. She wouldn't want us to lose focus. So, she's got a month, and then I'll go and kick her butt."

Sawyer nodded, tears running down her face, and my brother pulled her into his arms. When he looked up to where I placed the camera, I jumped, feeling like he'd caught me. But he couldn't know? Could he?

Either way, I quickly exited, shoving my computer off my lap like that made a difference. At least I'd learned I had a couple of weeks to make some plays before they came for me. It was more than I thought I'd get. The urge to not let them down filled me, and I jumped off the bed, putting the few items I had spread out around the room back into my bag. I picked up my trash and straightened the bed a little.

Grabbing my computer to put it in my bag, I opened it up to check one last thing and found that Blackhawk had responded.

Blackhawk: Oh, this and that. Just keeping things in order. You know how it is.
Blackhawk: Hey, listen, I actually have a job I could use your help on. Interested?

Seemed my luck was finally turning. Before I slipped the laptop back into the case, I replied, feeling a piece of the puzzle click into place. Slinging my bag over my shoulder, I dumped out the envelope that had been shoved under the door, picking up the car keys and putting them in my pocket. A fake ID and prepaid debit card laid on the bed, warming my heart at Milo's thoughtfulness. He truly was so much more than his lineage.

Pocketing them as well, I crumpled the envelope and tossed it into the trash before glancing around, taking in my surroundings once last time. This was it. The moment I stepped out of this room, I was no longer Finley Amelia Reyes but Oblivion. I couldn't stop until I took Blackhawk down, and only then could I return to being the woman I wanted to be.

Oblivion: Depends. Will you be there? I'm heading to a new location, so I'll be off the grid for a day. Send me the details, and I'll look them over. XOXO

Five

ASA

THE WAVES CRASHED against the shore, not bringing me the sense of calm they typically did. I'd been sitting in the sand, staring out into the ocean, trying to figure out what to do. In the past, I'd come out here when I had a hard decision to make, and the sounds of the waves as I surfed soothed me, bringing what I needed to do to the surface, casting all the other junk away.

But today was the same as yesterday, which was the same as the days before. It had been one week since I'd found Fin's letter and had my heart ripped out of my chest. One week since we'd joined our bodies together, consummating our love for one another in a way we hadn't before. One week since I'd felt like I no longer had a direction to go in. One week since my world had stopped.

What I hated the most was how I hadn't realized how much I loved her until it happened. We'd exchanged "I love you" before, but for some reason, I hadn't known what that truly felt like until it was gone. A gaping hole sat in my chest now, and I didn't know how to fill it so I could be whole again without her.

Giving up on the ocean being a mind whisperer, I fell back onto the sand, staring up at the darkening sky. When my phone buzzed in my pocket, I pulled it out, hoping it would be her. Sighing at the screen, I answered it as I stared off.

"Hey, Mom."

"How you doing, hun?"

I let out a long breath, rubbing my eyes. "Not so great. The ocean hasn't brought me the same clarity as usual. I don't know how to wait for her to finish whatever she wants to do. I feel like if I don't go after her, then I'll lose her forever. But that would be going against her wishes, and I don't want to do that."

"Asa, honey, I love you so much, and you've become a great man. In your efforts to be the complete opposite of Orson, though, you might have taken the perfect thing a little too far, and I'm saying that as your mother who loves you dearly. It's okay to break a rule, to go after what you want, to say hell with it all, and be selfish for once in your life."

"I...." I swallowed, feeling slightly shocked by my mother.

"I know. It's not what you expect me to say, but honey, take it from someone who didn't go after her heart and settled. Time goes by too quickly. In many ways, Samson thought he could do one job and return to me, but it ended up being more complex than he could've ever imagined. At that point, he felt committed to staying the course. Don't let that happen to Fin. I know how you feel about her and how she feels about you. Go. After. Her."

"It's that simple?"

"Yes. Fin is brilliant, but she's also stubborn. She probably thinks she's doing you a favor by shielding you, but all she's doing is keeping herself from experiencing joy. You just have to show her you're more tenacious and can get your hands dirty." She paused, taking a breath, and I knew she was gearing up to tell me something I might not want to hear. "I think Cohen could help you."

"Oh, um, I dunno."

It wasn't that I didn't want his help. There was just this weird tension since the whole incident when Fin had been kidnapped by the Council that made it awkward. But maybe that was just on me? He was working with Samson now, so that had to mean he was good.

"What does Sam—, I mean Dad, think?"

"Honey, no one is forcing you to call him Dad. We both know you didn't grow up knowing he was your father, and the man who claimed to be wasn't worthy of the title. He and Sawyer had a previous relationship, so it was easier for her. It took her a while to call me mom, and I didn't rush her. It will be better when it's natural for you and him. So, don't feel guilty about it at all."

Sighing, I rubbed my face, spreading sand over my forehead. I'd forgotten I'd been playing with it as I sat staring out into the ocean for answers.

"Yeah, I know."

Standing up, I dusted off my pants and shook the sand from my clothes. Usually, the sand didn't bother me because the surfing was worth it. When all I did was sit in it, I found it a bit of a nuisance.

"As for Samson, he thinks Cohen is probably already looking into it more despite Henry saying to stop. He thinks Cohen has a bit of a crush on Fin. Is that why you hesitate to reach out? Are you feeling unsure of your role in her life?"

It might be weird to talk about your love life with your mom for some people, but it wasn't for me. My mom and I were super close, only having each other growing up, and I shared practically everything with her.

"I don't know what it is. When I met him, it was after she'd been taken. He came in cocky, and I didn't know how to take him. Since then, I know they've worked on a few things, but she was always cautious in choosing her words and didn't say much about it. I kept waiting for her to bring it up. Even Sawyer said something to me, but Fin never did, so I guess I shoved it aside, figuring I didn't have to look at that piece too closely if she wasn't going to."

I started to head back to the beach house I was staying in; the sun almost set at this point. My stomach growled, reminding me I was hungry as well and I would need to figure something out to eat.

"I don't know what it feels like to love more than one person romantically at a time, but I know your sister does, and she makes it work. If you're struggling, talk to one of the guys. Ollie and Ty would know how you're feeling. I'm not saying you'll find yourself in a similar situation, but if you're worried about it, I think you'll feel better if you have all the information. You were always one who liked to be prepared as a child."

Climbing the stairs that led to the back of the property, I thought about what she said and how right she was. I didn't do well with uncertainty. Even if this wasn't the direction my life went in, maybe I needed to figure out if I could be okay with it first, and there was no time like the present to do that. Fin was hiding, giving me the perfect time to figure out my own mind and heart.

"You're absolutely right, Mom. Thanks. I'll give Cohen a call and see if he has any leads. It's a good place to start."

"I'm so glad I could help. I've been worried about you. Let me know if you need anything else. I love you, Son."

"Love you too, Mom."

I ended the call, sliding it back into my pocket as I walked over to the water pump. Turning it on, I rinsed my feet and shins free of sand. I snagged a towel off the rail that had been lying in the sun, and I dried my feet as I hopped into the back door.

Walking into the kitchen, I debated if I wanted to fix something or order in tonight before I dug my head out of my ass and called the one person I should've called from the start.

"I ordered some Chinese food," a voice said as I turned on the overhead light.

"Jesus Christ!" I shouted, jumping back at the sound. When I realized I wasn't about to be attacked, I stopped, holding the doorway as my heart returned to normal.

"Why am I not surprised you're here?" I said, bending at the waist as I peered at him.

"Have you been thinking about me, pretty boy?" he teased.

He slid off the barstool he'd been perched on and walked toward me. As he neared, I took in his tall frame, disheveled dark blond hair, and the wrinkles on his clothes. Cohen could tease all he wanted, deny he felt more for Fin than just a friend, but the facts were staring at me in the face. I could either be brave and face them like my mom suggested or keep my head buried in the sand, potentially losing her forever.

Since I was finding I had a strong dislike for sand, I think it was time to face this obstacle head-on and discover where that left me.

"I was actually going to call you. We need to talk." I righted myself, placing my hands on my hips as I stared him down. He wasn't a skinny nerd like you'd think a tech genius would be, but my years of hockey had him beat on the muscle side.

"Oh?" He stopped his forward approach, and leaned back against the counter, crossing his arms. "You know, when I broke into your house, I thought it would be harder to get you to listen to me." He smiled like he'd already won. "Go on, what do you have to say?"

"I want to help you find Fin, and I think we should talk about your feelings for my girlfriend."

He stared at me, his eyes searching for something. He wasn't teasing or making light of the situation for once, showing me he could be serious when needed.

"Now, I'm really glad I ordered Chinese food. This will be a better conversation over some noodles and rice."

Relaxing, I walked to the fridge and pulled out two beers, handing him one. "So, where do we start?"

Cohen smiled, and I realized I didn't hate the guy. In fact, he was pretty easy to get along with when he wasn't incessantly flirting with me. The doorbell rang just as my stomach growled again, and I was thankful it was one less decision I'd have to make tonight.

As he paid the delivery person and placed copious amounts of food on the table, I sat down, feeling more clear than I had all week. It seemed the ocean had helped to at least bring me to the place I needed to be to face what I'd been hiding from.

"I have an idea of where she is and how we can intercept her," Cohen said, scooping out some food.

"You have my attention."

He handed me a carton, and I began to eat, listening to his plan. When he finished, I nodded, wiping my mouth.

"I'm in. Now, how do you feel about Fin?"

Six

FINLEY

TWO WEEKS HAD PASSED and I had nothing to show for my time away except a mild addiction to vending machine mini donuts. Blackhawk had been quiet the past week, and I wondered if he'd somehow caught wind of my thoughts and knew what I was up to. Not that I was up to much of anything other than becoming a slob.

Looking around my new hotel room, I realized how disgusting I'd become. Wrappers littered the floor, soda bottles tumbled out of the trash can, and the few outfits I had were strewn about.

"Jeez, I've turned into Henry," I mumbled. Since I only had myself for company, I'd gotten used to talking aloud so I wouldn't feel so alone. I avoided thinking how sad that was.

Heaving myself off the bed, I sniffed my shirt, the

stench making my nose curl up. I smelled worse than my brother's gym bag.

Okay, first things first, I needed to clean up. I couldn't think in this pigsty. No wonder I hadn't made any progress. I'd fallen into a rabbit hole and forgotten to check for light every now and then. Shoving all the wrappers into a new trash bag, I sat it and the one with bottles outside my door. Opening the curtains, I squinted as the sun filtered into the room, shining some light into the dark space. Tiny dust particles floated around, making it even more obvious I needed to get out of this room. I was becoming one with the dust.

Grabbing all of my clothes, I shoved them into a laundry bag. I'd have to figure something out there. I hadn't thought the limited amount of outfits through when I'd packed. I was tired of wearing the same three things. Even off the grid, I still wanted my fashion, it seemed.

"You can take the girl out of fashion school, but you can't take fashion out of the girl," I chided, laughing at myself.

Okay. I was losing it. Perhaps a stroll to get food would be wise. Nodding my head, I made my way to the bathroom, determined to make myself clean.

Thirty minutes later, I smelled better and felt like a human again. Placing a blonde wig on my head, I pulled out some makeup and applied eyeliner and lipstick. Stepping away from the mirror, I found a new version of myself staring back.

"Time to be a badass," I whispered.

Grabbing my bag of dirty clothes, I'd head to the front desk to see if they had any laundry services. I wasn't expecting much, but it never hurt to ask. The elevator was quiet as it descended, and I quickly made it to the bottom floor. The nice thing about this hotel was how empty it seemed to be. Probably not for them, but it worked well for me wanting to stay hidden.

"Good afternoon, ma'am. How can we help you today?" the lady at the desk asked. God, I loved the south and their hospitality.

"Um, yes, I wondered if you had laundry services or knew a nearby place?"

"There's a laundromat around the corner open 24-7. Would you like me to draw you a map?" she asked.

"Sure, that'd be helpful." I'd been hoping they had one on-site so I wouldn't have to sit with them. But it was better than dirty clothes. I'd have to grab some more in the meantime.

Taking the paper, I stepped out of the hotel, shielding my eyes from the sun. I looked left and right and decided to go right first. A few food places were open already, and people went to and fro. I spotted the laundromat and peeked in, checking out the establishment.

Continuing on my walk, I found a little boutique a few feet further down that snagged my interest. Stepping into it, I was able to find a few things to add to my wardrobe and help me not run out of clothes as quickly. Feeling energized by the new threads, I decided to grab some food and eat there, hoping the social interaction would be good for me. I'd never been one to be a hermit, so going two weeks without interacting with more than the housekeeper was starting to get to me.

A bar a block over caught my eye, so I stepped in, blinking as my eyes adjusted to the darker environment. The place wasn't busy since it was late afternoon, so I made my way to the bar and placed my bags on an empty stool. It felt easier to sit at the bar since I was alone. I looked out into the space, people watching as I waited for the bartender to walk over.

"What can I get you, doll?"

"I'd like the cheeseburger. Hold the onion with a side of onion rings. And the largest Diet Coke you have."

He stopped, raising his eyebrows. "Hold the onion, but onion rings?"

"Yep." I nodded, not feeling I needed to explain myself. He laughed, shaking his head.

"They taste different," a rich voice said as they sat on a barstool over from me.

I turned toward the sound, finding myself ensnared in deep chocolate eyes. They reminded me of chocolate brownies with a layer of caramel mixed in. I tried to catch the gold strands, but they seemed to move with the light. That was when I realized I'd been staring at this guy, moving my head to see his eyes better.

Placing my head on my hand, I pretended to have been looking for a spot to put my elbow. "Exactly. He gets it," I said, turning back to the bartender to find he was no longer there. "Hmph."

Patting the counter, I tried to ignore the chuckle I could hear next to me. I did not need to turn and acknowledge him. Nope. I did not need to. With a strength I didn't know I possessed, I managed to keep my gaze focused straight ahead for a solid minute.

When I finally gave in to the urge to turn, I let out a breath, realizing I'd been holding it simultaneously. It sputtered over my lips, making the guy laugh.

"Easy there."

His voice sounded like he was perpetually laughing at you, keeping a secret only he knew. I could tell he was the type of guy that would ruin me, and for once, I was glad I wasn't on the market. Well, I hoped I wasn't.

The knowledge that Asa was out there made my mood drop, and I turned back to the front, this time having no difficulty keeping my gaze there.

"Sorry if I offended you," the guy said a few minutes later, a hint of remorse in his voice I wasn't expecting.

"No, I just remembered someone I miss."

"Ah. Far from home?"

"Yes, but don't think you can kidnap me, and no one would notice. Because they would. In fact, I have to check in every 30 minutes, so, yeah." I crossed my arms, lifting my chin. *Try to steal me now, potential kidnapper.*

He chuckled, holding his hands up in a placating gesture. "No plans to kidnap you here. But that's good to know about the check-in. That's smart."

When he acknowledged my thinking, it did something to me. A fluttery feeling beneath my breastplate began to emerge, and I found my cheeks heating. Ah, sugar sticks, I was blushing. I didn't need to be blushing over a random guy.

Clearing my throat, I pulled out my phone to pretend it was time to check-in. It seemed to work as he didn't interrupt me again. My food came out a few minutes later, and I dug in, realizing how starved I was. Those vending machine donuts only went so far.

"I'm impressed," the guy said when I'd cleared my plate, only a burned onion ring left behind.

Shrugging, I decided it was better to not engage with this guy to save myself from embarrassment. I waved the bartender over once I was done, ready to put some distance between the too handsome stranger with the deep voice and magic eyes and me.

"Can I grab my check?"

"Sure thing. Do you need anything else?"

"Nope. I'm going to run to the little girls' room, but I'll be back."

He tapped the bar as I slid off, walking down the little hallway with my bags. If I was going to sit and wait for things to be clean, I'd better wash them all. Slipping on the new things, I tossed the tags into the trash and turned in the mirror, checking them out. I'd gone with a simple blue jean skirt that had some rips in it and a navy-blue sleeveless polka-dotted shirt that had a cute bow in the front. It paired well with my Chucks. I looked cute. Not that I was trying to impress anyone. Nope.

Grabbing everything, I walked out and relaxed when I saw the guy was no longer at the bar. I sighed, even if I was a little disappointed he was gone. Looking for the receipt, I realized there wasn't anything in my spot either.

Motioning for the bartender, I waved him over. He looked at me oddly, probably realizing I'd changed.

"Can I help you, ma'am?"

"Um yeah, I thought you were getting my check for me?"

"Oh, the guy you were with paid for them both. He said he'd wait for you outside." The bartender looked at me funny like I was the one imagining things.

"What?" I asked, even though I'd heard him clearly. He started to explain again when I waved him off, turning to walk out. Shielding my eyes from the brightness of the sun, I looked in both directions, but didn't see anyone.

Why on earth would he pay for my meal? I couldn't let the thought go, and I thought about it all through the next few hours as I sat at the laundromat waiting for my clothes to dry.

Just who was that guy?

A FEW DAYS LATER, I finally had a response back from Blackhawk, and now indecision and regret sat heavy in my belly. I needed to make sure that I didn't lose myself in the hunt this time. That I didn't let my need to be right or prove I was smarter make me lose everything I had waiting back in Utah for me. I refused to think they wouldn't be there. So for now, I was happy in denial mode, believing everything would work out if I could just show Blackhawk he wasn't as good as he thought he was.

Blackhawk: So, that job? You interested?
Oblivion: Yep. Where have you been?
Blackhawk: I had something come up. It's not important.
Oblivion: Because that's not cryptic.
Blackhawk: Are you wanting to play our game, little hacker? A trade for a trade?

Thoughts of nights spent trading secrets rushed me, and I tried to blink them back, but they filled my mind with teenage angst and longing. Blackhawk was too charming. He had been from the start.

FINLEY, AGE 16

C:/Enter your name
C:/Oblivion

C:/Welcome Oblivion. You will be assigned to a team.

An email popped up with a web address. Clicking on it, I was directed to a closed server on the dark web. My fingers itched to type as I waited for others to populate the chat. Adrenaline pumped through me that I'd made it this far.

I didn't want to seem too eager, so I sat back as they started to chat, observing their interaction so I could know how to play it.

Mongoose: Hi. Is this our team?

Blackhawk: Hi Goose? Can I call you Goose? Yes, looks like it's the four of us.

Obsidian: Really? Why must you always be in the same chats as me?

Blackhawk: Because my awesomeness makes up for your boringness.

Obsidian: That doesn't make sense. You're the worst.

Obsidian: See, you scared the other member away.

Blackhawk: Nah, that was your lameness.

Blackhawk: Hi. Don't be scared. He's mostly harmless.

Oblivion: I'm not scared. I'm just observing you guys like animals in a zoo.
Blackhawk: Oh, what animals are we?
Obsidian: Great, you're both dumb. Can we get to business and leave the animal talk for another time? Preferably when I'm not there.
Oblivion: Sure, sour puss. You'd definitely be a baboon, by the way.
Blackhawk: Okay, Oblivion. You're cool. I like your wit.
Obsidian: Our first task is to infiltrate a business and create a dummy account without being detected. I'll handle logistics. Hawk, you got security? What're your skill sets Oblivion and Mongoose?

Panic rushed through me. They seemed so much more professional than me. I could tell this wasn't their first time. I needed to sound like I was competent.

Oblivion: Um, hacking.

Crap that did not sound smart! That didn't even sound confident.

Obsidian: Fine, play it cool. I'll give you a job, and you'll just have to deal with it.

Phew, that somehow worked.

Obsidian signed off.

Private message from Blackhawk.

Blackhawk: Okay, so realness here. You have no idea what he was asking do you?
Oblivion: Was it that obvious? This is my first time joining something like this.
Blackhawk: Sid assumes everyone is a smartass, so you're good on that front, and Mongoose just seems along for the ride. What's your hacking skill?
Oblivion: Why should I tell you? What's in it for you?
Blackhawk: Fine, how about a trade. A secret for a secret? We don't know one another, so what's the harm in sharing?

I THOUGHT about it and realized he was right. He didn't know me, so I could be honest with him without it costing too much.

Oblivion: Okay. I'm interested. But you owe me two since you already know one thing about me—that I'm clueless.

Blackhawk: Budding extortionist. I like it. Fine. One secret to even us out. I'm scared of the dark and have to sleep with a night light.

Oblivion: Wow. I'm speechless.

Blackhawk: I know. It's a shocker for most people.

Oblivion: I'm rolling my eyes so hard I hope you can feel them.

Blackhawk: Okay, spill. Why are you here if it's your first club initiation?

Oblivion: I'm not sure what my hacking skill area is. I taught myself and took a few classes. I'm here because I want to find out information about a friend.

Blackhawk: What things have you done well? What did you use as your entrance piece?

Oblivion: I created a way for teenagers to mask their location so their parents don't know where they are. Is that a thing?

Blackhawk: Yes, that's pretty badass. It sounds like Bait and Switch then. Just say that if someone asks.

Oblivion: Thank you. Your turn.

Blackhawk: I was hoping you'd forget that part. Fine.

Blackhawk: Hacking is the only thing that I'm good at. There I said it.

Oblivion: How is that possible? Shouldn't you be good at math and other things, then?

Blackhawk: You'd think that, but no. Nothing else sticks but hacking. I can do it in my sleep.

Oblivion: Wow, that's kind of sad.

Blackhawk: Geez, thanks. Well, I gotta go. Time to turn on the night light. Be good, kid.

Oblivion: I'm not a kid!

Blackhawk: Sure.

Blackhawk signed off.

PRESENT DAY

From that point forward, a trade was established, and we shared secrets back and forth like mono. Him bringing it up again was like a stab to my heart that I wasn't ready for.

Oblivion: No trade. What's the job?

Blackhawk: You're no fun anymore. Fine. I need one of your specialties. A Trojan horse.

Oblivion: Done. Send me the specs.

Blackhawk: Ah, no chatting?

Oblivion: I have nothing to say to you. I need the job. That's it. I'll send you my banking information too. I want to be paid half upfront.

Blackhawk: Fine. I'll send it over. You're not as fun anymore.

Oblivion signed off.

My heart hammered, and I was sure it was about to beat out of my chest. I hadn't gained as much information as I wanted, but it was a start. The worst part was that I hadn't expected jumping back into this role would be so difficult. Especially when memories kept flooding me. I needed to find him soon and end this before I forgot why I was tracking him in the first place.

THE ALARM STARTED TO BLARE, *and I cursed as I twisted the lock pick to the right. It had been easy to break into my room when I'd practiced, but this office building was causing more problems than I'd anticipated. I took a deep breath and twisted the pick again, finally hearing the satisfying click as the door unlocked. Wiping my brow, I skirted into the room and raced to the alarm panel.*

"Guys, you there?" I asked, tapping the phone app Blackhawk had developed for us to use to chat while in the field. It disguised our voices and location but allowed us to have real-time access to one another.

"Yeah, that was close," Obsidian said. Even though his voice was masked, I could still hear the reprimand he wanted to give me. I'd come to feel Obsidian didn't respect me, but I didn't take it personally. He didn't respect

anyone, from what I could gather. "If you get caught, you're on your own."

"Gee, thanks," I huffed, rolling my eyes.

"You know we wouldn't do that," Blackhawk said. The only reason I knew it was him was the familiar kindness in his voice. Our games of trading secrets had become a regular thing, and I was beginning to understand the mysterious hacker on a real level, unlike the other two.

"Mongoose, you ready with the alarm key?" I asked, popping the panel off.

"Yeah, it's, um, 85923."

Typing in the code, I held my breath as I waited to see if it worked. I only had another minute before the police would be dispatched.

Error flashed up on the screen, and my nerves racketed up. I was beginning to regret volunteering to be the one to go out into the field. It had felt like a good option at the time to make myself valuable to the team. I wouldn't admit it because I was too nervous to say I didn't know how to do the other things. Nope. Obsidian didn't need another reason to hate me.

"Um, that didn't work. Do you have another one?" I asked, some of the anxiety creeping up my voice, making it high-pitched to the point I wasn't sure the app could mask it.

"Hold on, Oblivion. I got you," Blackhawk soothed, calming me by his mere presence.

"That's another strike, Mongoose," Obsidian yelled. "One more, and you're off the team."

"I… I'm sorry. It should work. He must've updated it or something."

"Can you save the bickering for later and give me the fucking code already! I'm this close to being arrested, and I'm too pretty for prison," I shouted, stopping their argument.

"Type in 85932," Blackhawk said. Trusting him, I typed it in, holding my breath. I looked around for the closest exit. Thankfully, this one worked.

"See, I just had the last numbers inverted," Mongoose argued. Obsidian and he started to go back and forth, and I couldn't take their distraction anymore, so I muted the channel, focusing on my task.

Scanning the room, I looked for the thing I'd come for. When smoke began to fill the space, I coughed, not understanding. Turning, I was met with a purple elephant and a polka-dotted bear chasing me down the hallway as I searched for a window. Sounds of shouting followed me as I jumped.

Sitting up, I gasped for breath, the nightmare having felt too real. My skin felt clammy, and my neck was sweaty. The AC kicked on, rattling to life, and I jumped, the sound scaring me but bringing me more into the present. Goosebumps rose up on my skin, and I rubbed my arms.

"You're here. You're not there. It's in the past." I rocked back and forth as I said the statement repeatedly, trying to rebury a night from my past I'd rather forget.

Once I'd calmed down, I looked over at the nightstand, reading the clock. *4:00 am.* No time like the present to get started on revenge. The nightmare was a good reminder of what was at stake. Climbing out of bed, I took a quick shower to clean off the remnants of the dream. Sitting down at my computer, I got to work. I could sleep when I was back with my friends and family.

A FEW DAYS LATER, I'd been able to trace the link that Blackhawk had sent me, but it led to a dummy IP address. I knew he was better than that to lead me straight to him, but I hoped he'd be lax enough not to go through the effort of cloaking his location.

"Guess I'll have to trust that he's not sending me into a trap," I mumbled, getting dressed. Sliding on the leather pants I'd left the house in, I paired them with one of the new tops I'd gotten, my black heels, and a black jacket. I looked like a real Femme Fatale, helping me lean into the part I was playing.

Throwing some essentials into my messenger bag,

I picked up the few things in the room, working harder to keep it clean. I reminded myself how much nicer it would feel to come back to a clean room afterward. Checking my watch again, I adjusted my glasses and headed out. No time like the present.

Sitting outside a dry cleaners a few hours later, I began to wonder if I'd encoded the coordinates wrong. The bus bench had grown warm throughout the day, but it was beginning to become colder with the sun setting. Sitting on metal in the cold was not really my forte, and these pants did nothing to hold in the warmth. When another ten minutes went by, and there was still no activity from the dry cleaners, I decided to move into the cozy coffee shop on the corner. I'd have a more angled view of this place, but I didn't think it would matter all that much. I was pretty certain I'd been had. I was just too stubborn to admit it.

Slinging my bag onto my shoulder, I ducked my head from the cameras, adjusting the pink wig I was sporting today. I kept changing my looks, hoping it would buy me some time before the others found me.

Entering the coffee shop, the few guests ignored me, all too busy on their own computers, as I made my way to the counter. Quickly, I ordered a cookie and lemonade, deciding the last thing I needed right now was caffeine. I was jittery enough on my own. The tapping foot as I waited was a clear indicator.

The waitress eyed me but didn't say anything as she handed me my order. She probably thought I was a junkie. Oh well.

Taking my goodies, I scouted out a place near the front window that was semi-private, allowing me to have my back to the wall so no one could see my screen. I needed to use the free Wi-Fi and didn't need nosey people peeking over my shoulder trying to guess what I was doing.

As I settled, no one had even glanced over at me, so maybe I was among my people and wouldn't need to worry. I checked on the dry cleaners but still found it dark and empty.

I was to look for a man with a cowboy hat. Once I made contact with him, then he'd give me something. Blackhawk hadn't said what, just that I would know when I saw it.

It had taken me a few days to get to this sleepy town of South Carolina. I didn't know if it was where Blackhawk was or just where his contact was going to be. It was strange traveling this much on my own. I was so used to always being part of a pair with Henry, or Sawyer, and then Asa. Being here as just Fin felt odd, but I didn't hate it as much as I'd expected. I was learning new things about myself, which was the good part.

Checking one more time for the mysterious man, I signed into a secure server to see if I could do any more leg work on just who Blackhawk was. I realized that finding him physically was much harder than I'd anticipated. While I'd tracked him down online, it meant nothing if I couldn't see him face to face to exact my revenge.

Though, I had to admit my plan on what I was going to do when that step came was just as shoddy. I really had jumped into this with both feet, not even looking to see where I was landing. Which was both good and bad.

Good, because typically, I was so anal about things it made everyone around me bonkers.

Bad, because the longer this took me, the more time I missed away from my boyfriend and friends.

It was time to let some of my "Finleyness" out to roam. I needed to be more prepared, so when I got to the end of this revenge list, I knew how it ended.

Before my big scandal, the one I tried to not think about anymore, I'd been working on a program to find Sariah. I just needed to tweak it and add the information I knew about Blackhawk, and then maybe I'd have better luck finding him.

Signing in to the program was easy, and I found

my fingers typing in the familiar code as the prompts came up. Every now and then, I'd peek up to make sure the contact wasn't there, but I still had no sign of the man. I passed the security measures with one last prompt, and I found myself in the program.

The familiar page stared at me, and emotions I hadn't felt in years began to permeate my being. I'd been such a lost and confused teenager, and staring at the screen, I remembered how desperate I'd been to feel something, anything other than the emptiness inside me.

It had been a hopeless recklessness that led me to my choices, and I briefly wondered if I was repeating the same pattern of mistakes as I had back then.

I didn't dwell on that for too long, shoving everything back into the depths of my mind where it belonged. I could dive into those thoughts later when I had the time, but now I needed to focus. Glancing up one more time, I almost missed the man I'd been waiting all day to see.

I'd been expecting to see nothing, so I had to look twice to catch the black cowboy hat as it moved away from the door and around the alley.

"Fudge!" I hissed, jumping up and slinging my bag over my shoulder as I grabbed my computer in one hand. I knocked into a few chairs, startling the other customers, but I couldn't focus on it, needing to get outside before I lost the contact. While I'd been happy with my corner for privacy earlier, I cursed it now as I tried to make my way around bags and legs to get to the door.

The humid air hit me as I made it outside, and I dashed across the street as fast as possible, once again cursing my selected footwear. "Why do I keep insisting on wearing heels?" I muttered as I careened around the corner, catching sight of the man as he ducked into a door.

I clicked and clacked down the alley toward the door as fast as I could. Lurching forward, I grabbed the handle a millisecond before it closed. I stood with it in my grasp for a second, amazed it had worked. Realizing I was losing time, I pulled it back and slid in, stopping as my eyes began to adjust to the darkness. It looked like the back of a bar or club, the kegs and boxes of beer along one side cluing me in. I began to make my way down the hall, watching for random boxes as I went.

Movement further down the hallway caught my eye, and I stepped around cases and bottles as I tried to catch up to him again. I didn't know if I should make myself known and call out to him or just follow at a distance. I needed to get more information from Blackhawk next time.

"Next time?" I admonished myself, realizing how

quickly I'd seemed to have lost the plot. I was here to stop him, not join his club of illegal activities.

Music and voices grew louder the further down the hall I went, so I wasn't surprised when I turned and found myself in a dive bar. The only problem, the bar was full of men with cowboy hats.

I stood there, mouth open, trying to find the one I'd been chasing. "What? How? Huh?"

"You okay there, darling?" a southern drawl asked. Turning, I found a woman dressed in short shorts and a flannel shirt tied at her waist.

"Um, I was meeting someone, and they came in here, but now I can't find them. Is there something going on?"

"It's Friday night," she said, like that explained it.

"Right. Tourist," I said, pointing. She laughed a little and then pointed at a sign that read "Friday Night Square Dancing."

"If you're staying, you better pair up quick before all the good ones are taken. You don't want to get stuck with handsy Steve." She pointed to a man who looked like he barely had any teeth and smiled over at us.

Doing a full-body shudder, I thanked the woman and made my way to the bar. Maybe if I sat there, I'd be able to find the one guy in a cowboy hat I was supposed to meet. Sounded plausible.

Shoving my laptop back into my bag, I zipped it and squeezed between two couples at the end. The only open stool was sticky, and I hoped it was only from spilled drinks. Perching on it carefully, I looked out into the crowd, surveying all the men with black hats.

After twenty minutes, I realized the futility of trying to find one person in a bar full of people who all looked alike. It was impossible. Especially when I didn't even know his name or what he looked like. Sighing, I slumped off the stool, ignoring the squelching sound, and walked toward the door. I was only a few feet away when a waitress collided with me, spilling her tray of drinks all over me.

"Son of a biscuit!"

"I'm so sorry, hun. Here, let me help you." She started to pat me dry with the cocktail napkins, but it was of no use. I was covered from head to toe in the sticky substance.

"Don't bother." Dropping my head, I sulked out of the bar as everyone watched me. I felt humiliated, but at least I had the good fortune that no one knew me. The biggest inconvenience was the fact that this was my last set of clean clothes. Looked like another long night at the laundromat. Sighing, I trudged along. Each step was crucifying as I made a sticky sound when my feet lifted from the pavement. I was so consumed with my situation I didn't see the man outside the bar leaning against the wall until I practically ran into him.

"Ma'am," he said, startling me. His voice sounded familiar, but I couldn't make out any features with most of his face in the shadow, hidden below his cowboy hat.

"Sorry, sir. I wasn't paying attention."

"I believe I'm to give you this." He held out an envelope, placing it in my hand. "Good day."

He was gone before I could call out to him, my body frozen to the spot at my luck. Had he seen me inside? How did he know who I was but not the other way around?

Opening my bag, I realized too late that the contents of it were now sodden and bright red. I was too upset to check my computer; the device's fate was pretty much guaranteed to be ruined.

Trudging back to the hotel, I tried to come up with possible outcomes and solutions. But I had to face the facts. I was woefully unprepared, and the only thing I had succeeded at was being covered in a sticky mess. Not even the fun kind.

Maybe it was time to call it quits. I'd been wrong. I wasn't cut out for this. It was just another area of my life that I failed at.

I'd gotten so good at pretending I had it all

together, I'd almost convinced myself the same, but the reality was, I had no idea what I was doing or where to go from here. It was time to throw in the towel and face the facts.

Finley Reyes was a loser. I'd known it at seventeen, and it was still true, six years later.

TEARS STREAMED DOWN my face as I stared at the destroyed mess of my baby. There was no bag of rice big enough to save it from the liquid damage that tray of drinks had caused. It was toast, ruined.

And I'd never felt more lost in my life.

In a weird way, my computer had become my safety blanket, my emotional support. It had been there for me when everything felt too chaotic and out of reach, providing me with a way to try to find some answers or even some hope. That was why I'd joined the MidKnight Guild, to begin with. It was a place for me to connect with others who didn't know me as the little sister, or the screwup, and hopefully uncover the lies we'd been told about Sariah.

And it had been a safe haven for a while. Obsidian and Blackhawk had become my friends.

FINLEY, AGE 16

Obsidian: Has anyone heard from Mongoose? He missed another check-in.

Oblivion: No, I haven't. Did he ever send over the files from the mark he was working on?

Blackhawk: Yeah, I got them. He said he had some things to take care of in his personal life, but would be back on for the next task.

Obsidian: I wish someone would've told me. I'm team leader.

Blackhawk: Only because no one else wanted it. Don't get too high on yourself or I'll sic Oblivion on you.

Blackhawk: Speaking of, I can't believe you changed the name of the mean girl so that every teacher called her "Anita Hoare" on the first day of school roll call. That's hilarious and hardcore.

Oblivion: Been looking at my application again? Anyone ever tell you that you have some stalker tendencies?

Blackhawk: All the time. Don't ignore the compliment, little hacker.

Oblivion: That was a pretty great one. By the end of the day, her face was so red that I almost felt bad for her.

Obsidian: What about when you programmed the teacher's phone to make a moaning sound every time he got a message, Hawk? He never could figure out how to make it stop. Now, that was hilarious.

Blackhawk: That's because I disabled all of his settings. He was an asshole. Always trying to look down girls' tops and let the popular kids get away with whatever they wanted. It wasn't right. Especially when that one guy superglued your seat to your butt. He needed to be taught a lesson.

Oblivion: Wait? Do you guys know each other in real life? I just thought it was from other hacker clubs.

Obsidian: We've known each other for years, actually. We were placed in the same foster home for a while and then ended up at a group home around the same time.

Blackhawk: Yep, and now Sid is my roommate.

Oblivion: So, you're both in college? Or high school?

Obsidian: Getting a little too personal, Oblivion. We can share what we wish, but asking directly is frowned upon.

Blackhawk: Oblivion is cool, Sid. We can trust him. Yes, we're in college.

Oblivion: Well, if we're sharing information, then you should know I'm not a him, I'm a her.

Blackhawk: Really? That explains a lot, actually, but also badass, Oblivion.

Obsidian: Oh great, now Hawk will be obsessed with you. Before he starts mooning over the hacker chick, is everyone prepared for the next task?

Oblivion: Yep. I'm ready.

Blackhawk: I'm not mooning. Geez.

Blackhawk: But yes, your royal pain in my ass, I'm ready.

Obsidian: Good. We can't mess up another task. I'll see you all tomorrow at 22:30. Mongoose better be there or he's off the team.

Obsidian signed off.

Private message from Blackhawk.

Blackhawk: How do you feel about the task? You prepared? Do you need any help? I know things went a little haywire last time.

Oblivion: I'm good. That wasn't because of me. Why are you so invested?

Blackhawk: Something about you makes me want you to succeed. That's all, little hacker.

Oblivion: So, it's not because I have tits, and now you think I can't hack it?

Blackhawk: Oh, it's definitely because you have tits. But not in the way you're thinking.

Blackhawk: Sid can be an ass, but he wasn't lying. I already thought you were cool when I thought you were a guy. So, now, it's blowing my mind.

Oblivion: Um, not sure what to say now.

Blackhawk: Did I make it awkward? Sorry, I have a terrible habit of doing that.

Oblivion: No, it's just… guys don't really talk to me. So, I'm not sure how to take this. I feel like I'm about to walk into a bad '90s teen movie, and I'm some kind of bet.

Blackhawk: Well, kids at school are all schmucks. Everyone is trying to impress each other so that they don't take time to notice the actual cool people.

Oblivion: Speaking from experience?

Blackhawk: Maybe. I wasn't a jock, and being a foster kid made it more difficult to blend in. Remember, I'm horrible at school, and I have my whole bad-boy attitude going on for me, but I'm a nerd at heart. Shh, don't tell anyone.

Oblivion: You're secret's out now. I'm going to blackmail you so hard.

Blackhawk: Badass, Oblivion. Not that it would matter. College is a different game. I'm still not cool, but I found my people.

Oblivion: Hacker people?

Blackhawk: Some, like Sid, but just others who are intelligent and crafty.

Oblivion: You sound like you're building a nerdy gang.

Blackhawk: Maybe I am. Want to be part of it?

Oblivion: Sure, I'm your girl if you need someone to make you costumes.

Blackhawk: You're so much more than that, little hacker.

Oblivion: If you say so. Everything feels so bleak right now. The only light is this.

Blackhawk: Have you had any luck with your friend?

Oblivion: No. I'm beginning to wonder if maybe she is dead.

Blackhawk: I've heard of another hacker who might be able to help. Do you want his info?

Oblivion: Really? That would be awesome. Thank you.

Blackhawk: No problem. Just don't forget who your favorite hacker friend is.

Oblivion: Definitely, Obsidian.

Blackhawk: Oh, you hit me in my core. You know, I'm much prettier and smell better. I don't think the guy showers. You definitely don't want to be around that.

Oblivion: Mmm, BO, my favorite boy smell.

Blackhawk: Hey, little hacker, boys your age are dumb. Just saying.

Oblivion: Still convinced I'm a kid?

Blackhawk: No, but I know you're still younger than me.

Oblivion: Good thing we're just friends then. That's allowed, right?

Blackhawk: Sure thing, little hacker.

Blackhawk: I'll send you Chaos info. I've never talked to him, but I hear things, and he's good. Some brainiac already through school.

Oblivion: Thank you.

Blackhawk signed off.

PRESENT DAY

Staring at the screen, I blinked the memory away, not needing to add the loss and deception of my first real friends to the mix. Looking at my computer, it was almost sinister how it looked the same on the outside, but nothing remained the same on the inside. Kind of eerie how I was the same. Trying for the billionth time, I hit the on button, but nothing happened.

"Screw it," I sighed, closing the lid.

Pulling out my burner phone, I texted Blackhawk that I had an unfortunate computer malfunction, but I had the envelope and to let me know what he wanted me to do with it. I tossed the phone down as I laid back on the bed, and debated the same thing I did every night.

Was I making a mistake? It felt like it at this point. I had nothing to show for my efforts.

Maybe I had pushed all the blame onto him? These earlier memories of our friendship were clouding my judgment, making it difficult to remember the hurt and pain at the end. This was the problem with pushing your emotions down. You almost forgot the part that hurt.

Picking up my phone, I rolled over to my stomach and opened the cloud storage app I had. My thumb hovered over the photos icon and I clicked it, deciding a little pain might do me good.

Pictures of Asa and me, Sawyer and the BOSH crew, our time at TAS filled my screen as I flicked through them. When the album was done, it auto-matically opened the next one and I froze as screen-shots filled the screen. My mental shields were down, my security blanket gone, allowing the flashback to take over before I could stop it.

FINLEY, AGE 16

> **Obsidian**: Check the news.
> **Oblivion**: Why? What's going on?
> **Obsidian**: Just do it. I'll wait.

Rolling my eyes, I minimized the chat and clicked a new tab on the browser. My fingers hesitated as I tried to figure out what news source I should look up. Deciding to do a broad search, I typed in the local station and opened them in one tab, and one of the national news channels in another. Opening them both, I didn't have to scroll down far to find what I assumed he was talking about.

A building was on fire, and it was surrounded by emergency vehicles. Clicking on the video, I watched as the crews rushed to put it out to no avail. When a part of the structure fell, two people rushed out, a body slung over the arm of one of them. The reporter began talking and I only paid attention to parts of it as I searched the video for whatever clue Obsidian was referring to. He liked to send me tests to see if I could figure it out, so I had to assume this was one of those instances.

"... a teen body found... believed to be a club initiation... broken into... files stolen."

When the reporter said something about files, I zeroed in on her, giving her all of my focus. That was when I saw it, the tagline under her name.

Possible arson at the Magnolia House. An abandoned homeless shelter.

Bile rose up, and I pushed back my chair as I raced toward the bathroom. I managed to make it to the toilet as I heaved up my lunch and most of yesterday's contents as well.

"No, no, no, no, no," I cried, rocking back and forth. This couldn't be happening.

"Fin?" Henry yelled, stepping into my room. Quickly, I wiped my eyes and flushed the toilet, ridding it of my shame.

"Just a minute," I shouted, splashing some water on my face. It was time to be the perfect sister, not a possible homicidal hacker.

PRESENT DAY

Shaking my head, I cleared away the heavy fog of grief, shame, and regret that seemed to be my only companions these days. Wiping my eyes, I dropped the phone on the bed and rested my head on my arms. I hadn't thought about that night in years. I never did get to talk with Obsidian about it, and I supposed now I never would.

I laid on my arms for a while, lost in thoughts of what-ifs when the bed started to vibrate. I briefly wondered if I'd stumbled into one of those weird hotels and had a malfunctioning vibrating bed until I remembered I'd thrown down the burner. Moving my hand around, I searched for the device until I felt the hard shape in my hand. Pulling it to my face, I read the message across the screen.

Blackhawk: Open the envelope.

Sitting up, I reached over to the table I'd laid it on and dragged it to me. Ripping off the top, I peered inside, trying to figure out what it was. Sliding the paper and key out, I stared at the sheet, blinking, wondering if I had imagined things.

Want to play a game? Tag, you're it.

Blackhawk: Even with drinks spilled on you, you looked pretty, little hacker.

Oblivion: You were watching me? We're not going to get far in this job if you can't trust me.

Blackhawk: Confession time. I didn't have a job. I just wanted to meet you since you bailed on me all those years ago. I've been waiting for the opportunity for you to return. I've made the ultimate cat and mouse game for us.

Oblivion: Me? Bailed? I don't want to play your stupid game!

Blackhawk: That's too bad. If you change your mind, I'll be at the location for a while. If you can figure out the clue, you'll catch me first. If not, I'll leave you another.

Blackhawk: I've missed you. I'm glad you're back so we can play our games again. You'll want the prize at the end of this one.

Blackhawk: Game on, little hacker.

Rage coursed through me, and the earlier melancholy evaporated as a new emotion emerged.

Vengeance.

All the times I'd been made a fool of, all the situations at school where kids laughed at me, and all the little hoops I'd jumped through, it was never enough to prove my worth to any of them. I was tired of being the fool.

Fine. If he wanted to play a game, then we'd play.

Only this time, I wasn't a teenager with a crush. No, this time, I was a woman on a mission, and he just reminded me why.

Blackhawk acted like my friend, but he was a trickster, turning my whole world upside down for his own amusement. This time, I'd be the one laughing.

But first, I needed to make a phone call, or I wouldn't get anywhere.

My hand hovered over the keypad, but eventually, I made myself dial the number. As the phone rang, nerves skated up my arms, and I sucked in a breath as I waited for them to answer.

"Hello? Fin, is that you?"

"Hey. It's me. I, um, I need your help."

MILO CAME THROUGH AGAIN, sending me to a store to pick up a computer he ordered for me. I was going to owe him a few dinners at this rate. I told him I'd pay him back once I could use my bank account since I only had a limited amount of cash and the debit card he gave me. My budget hadn't included buying a new computer, but he told me not to worry about it. I didn't feel right taking something else from him, so I would either mail him the money, donate it in his name, or send him something of equal value. It felt like the right thing to do.

That and I didn't like owing people.

Taking the shiny computer out of the box felt close to an aphrodisiac. It was sleek, and I couldn't help but smile that he'd gone for the rose gold. I sat petting it for a few seconds, okay, a few minutes before I finally opened the screen and turned it on.

The speed it booted up was amazing, and I realized I might've needed a new one longer than I'd realized. Thankfully, I was neurotic about saving everything to three different cloud servers, so it didn't take long to log in and regain all my files. I didn't know if I would've been able to deal if I'd lost all the years of hacker programs I'd developed or had gleaned from others.

Actually, no, I definitely wouldn't have been able to deal. I would've curled into a ball and sobbed and then called my brother to come and rescue me.

At least this way, I was still trying to fight the fight and regain my sense of self. *As long as you avoid thinking about that place,* my subconscious whispered. And ignore.

My email box blinked at me, begging me to click on it, but I found a new email from Asa each time I gave in to checking it. I was too worried to see if they were "I hate you" emails or "I love you" ones to read them.

Yeah, chickenshit needed to be my middle name after loser.

Focusing on the code Blackhawk had left me, I plugged it into a program and then pulled up the one

I'd been working on before the whole "chase a cowboy" incident had left me in a sticky disaster.

Staring at the information needed, I realized I didn't have much to go on. I didn't know his real name. I knew he lived in the south at the time of initiation and was attending a state college with Obsidian. But I didn't know what he majored in or even if he had graduated. I didn't even know his eye or hair color. I would need to change the parameters to use this to find him.

Reaching into a new bag, I pulled out a pen and notebook. I'd had to replace them too, but fortunately, they were within my budget, and something I eagerly would shop for. Stationary was my jam.

Tapping the purple pen on the notebook, I tried to think of all the things I knew about Blackhawk.

College.

Foster care.

Roommates with Obsidian.

Scared of the dark.

Once bought me red stilettos.

~~Was funny and kind.~~ Nope, scratch that. He was annoying and an asshole.

Mid-twenties.

Not good at math.

Really good at staying hidden.

Part of a few hacker clubs.

Worked for some organization.

It was more than I'd had, but it wasn't a lot of identifying information. Based on how he'd covered himself at the bar with his cowboy hat, I couldn't even tell what his facial features were. Okay, so he was tall and had muscles. That was obvious. And his voice…

The realization hit me like a ton of bricks, and I knew why it had sounded familiar earlier. He'd been the guy at the bar, the one with the eyes I'd gotten lost in.

Nope, back that train up. I would not think the man who let me get arrested and ghosted me after had nice eyes. Big scoop of double nope.

So, what? He'd been following me for days? He knew who I was and how to locate me easily. Which meant his skills had improved, and I would be wasting my time trying to find a bread crumb if he didn't want me to.

But it also meant I had more information to enter into my database, and it might just be the thing that he didn't take into consideration.

Typing in dark hair, 6ft tall, brown eyes, light stubble, sharp jaw, well-built with muscles, and a deep voice into the search criteria, I realized I had just described every teenage heartthrob I had a crush on.

But surely, not all good-looking guys in their mid-twenties would have hacking skills. There had to be some criteria to filter out all the obvious people. I just had to keep digging.

Feeling slightly better and ignoring the mild attraction I had to the asshole, I switched over to the other program running through his code. When it beeped, I grinned, excited to have a location. Hopefully, he'd still be there four hours later, and I could end this tonight. But with the time it took for me to wallow and then go and get a new computer, my time might be up.

At least this time, I was prepared, and I'd be taking every precaution as I hunted his ass down.

He thought I was the mouse, but I'd show him he would be the one to fall into my trap in the end.

WALKING UP TO THE STOREFRONT, I debated if I should have just waited until morning. It was close to midnight now, and everything within a mile radius was closed, making the street eerily dark. The bookstore in front of me looked like an odd place for him to be, but I was confident in my program to have figured out his clue.

Cloak-N-Dagger Books looked like a regular bookstore, but after some hacking into their system and a thorough search on the dark web, I'd found they were actually a secret hangout for a club. I wasn't sure which club yet as that was all hush, hush. But the fact that it was more than meets the eye had me believing this was the right place. It was just like Blackhawk to pick something like this. He liked his puzzles, after all.

Walking down the alley, I looked for the brick with the X on it. It had been painted with black light paint, so I used the app on my phone to scan over all the bricks. I wasn't sure if they would make it a real big X or if it would be tiny, and I didn't want to miss it if it was.

Finding it halfway down, I pulled it out, where a key card slot was now revealed. Taking the card that Blackhawk had given me, I slid it in, holding my breath that it would work. I nearly jumped with joy when it beeped green a few seconds later. The door hissed open, and I tugged at it, amazed at how it pulled away from the other bricks. They'd done an excellent job of making it appear as part of the wall.

Stepping into the dark corridor, I suddenly felt dread hit me that maybe I should've told someone where I was. Just another reckless decision I kept making for the books. Huh, that was funny, considering I was in a bookstore.

Strolling through the store, I shook off my dark thoughts as my whole body came alive with energy at the realization I was closer than I'd ever been to finding him. This could be it, the night I had my vengeance and got to return to my family. Maybe it was that giddy deliriousness that had me not watching my steps.

As soon as I stepped over the threshold into the store, a loud sound erupted, something popping over my head seconds before I was covered in a liquid. A squeal left me as I sputtered. I stood, frozen, not sure what had just happened.

"Tsk, Tsk, little hacker. You're gonna have to up your game if you want to catch me. Better luck next time, babe," a recording said, playing through the speakers.

I blinked, wiping the wetness from my eyes. "What is it with people dumping shit on me today?" I screamed, my frustration coming out at last. Thank God I'd left my computer at the hotel this time. If I had destroyed two in one day, I would call it quits. Computer endangerment and all that.

Lights began to flicker in a pattern, annoying me even more. When I realized it was morse code, I ran over to the counter, grabbing the first thing I could find that I could write on. Which happened to be a roll of register paper, but it would work. Grabbing the pen, I started to write the dots and dashes down. It began to repeat after about a minute, so I stopped, staring at it. I guess this was my next clue.

I smiled, feeling alive in a whole new way. This was what we'd excelled at together. Back before, he betrayed me and broke my heart.

FINLEY, AGE 17

> **Blackhawk**: Okay, little hacker, if you were deserted on an island, who and what would you take with you?
> **Oblivion**: I'd obviously take that nature survivalist guy and a big machete. No one would mess with me with Beer and a big knife.
> **Blackhawk**: Ah, babe, you're so cute. You don't even realize it.
> **Blackhawk**: Also, wise choice, but he might take offense if you call him Beer.
> **Oblivion**: What? Why? Isn't that his name?
> **Blackhawk**: No, little hacker. I'll wait.

My cheeks flamed, but I couldn't deny how happy I was either. Blackhawk made me feel seen in a way I never had before. Googling, I quickly realized my mistake.

Oblivion: Well, I think it would be a joke between us because we'd be such good chums. Bear wouldn't mind at all.

Blackhawk: I could see that. You're probably right.

Blackhawk: You ready for a new puzzle? I've been working on it.

Oblivion: Oh, yes, give me! But first… I have a truth for a truth for you.

Blackhawk: Hit me with it. I live for these.

Oblivion: I feel sad for you if that's true.

Oblivion: Okay, my truth is that I sometimes hate that my brother gets to act broody, and my parents accept it, but if I show any emotion that isn't pleasant, I'm called out. I don't begrudge my brother, he lost someone too, but I hate that he's allowed to actually grieve it while I'm told to smile.

Blackhawk: That's understandable that you would feel that way, little hacker. I don't know the whole story, but I know how close to this person you were. It's not fair that you can't grieve however you see fit.

Oblivion: Thank you, that means a lot knowing I'm not crazy.

Blackhawk: Okay, I'll give you a truth somewhat similar. I kind of had the opposite thing. Everyone told me to feel sad when my mom died, but I didn't. She was abusive and consistently high. I was relieved. That's horrible of me, but it was how I felt.

Oblivion: So basically, people need to keep their feelings to themselves and quit telling us how to feel?

Blackhawk: Yep. That sounds about right.

Oblivion: Thanks for the laugh. Now, send me the puzzle. I'm eager to crack this one to prove to you my superiority.

Blackhawk: Good luck, babe.

Blackhawk: And anytime, little hacker. I'm here. Always.

PRESENT DAY

Stopping at the staff bathroom, I used some paper towels to get as much of what I was now sure was glow-in-the-dark paint off me. The part of me that wanted to stay and snoop around and find the secret underground club struggled to leave, but I knew I needed to get back to my computer and solve this next clue before I lost him again.

Trudging back to the hotel, I kept replaying all the times Blackhawk had been kind to me, a true friend. It was why it hurt the worst when he betrayed me. Obsidian had always been stern, and Mongoose, well, he didn't last long. In the end, it was Blackhawk who meant something to me and then he'd betrayed me.

I needed to confront him and find out why. I just wasn't sure if I was ready for the answer.

Stepping into the hotel room, the light flicked on, and I barely stopped myself from squealing for the second time tonight.

"I wondered when you would show up."

MOST PEOPLE probably had several moments they wished they could redo in their lives. Me, I only had one. That might sound arrogant, but I strove to lead a life of no regrets. And for the most part, I'd been successful, living my life to the fullest. If I wanted to kiss a boy, I did. If I wanted to kiss a girl, I did. If I wanted to fly to New York, I did.

Too much of my childhood had been limited, so I'd vowed to live a life of abundance when I could. And it had worked out, until her. The only mishap had been Finley Reyes—the girl with the magnetic eyes.

When I met her that first summer, I was enamored with her, but she was seventeen, so I put her firmly in the "do not think about" category. I hung out at her house a lot that summer and got to know her and Henry. Fin hadn't been around as much due to her community service obligations that summer, making it easier to ignore my attraction.

It took me longer than I'd like to admit to figure out she was Oblivion. Mostly because I had a massive crush on Oblivion and didn't want to reconcile that she was the seventeen-year-old daughter of my boss.

So when I discovered that the unattainable girl who made me curious was the same as the online hacker I'd befriended, I froze, not knowing what to do. So, I did what I did best and ignored the parts of my life that I didn't want to acknowledge.

I pretended it didn't matter. She hadn't met me, and I continued on with my flirting.

The moment her eyes landed on mine last year in that conference room, I felt the unmistakable regret I'd worked so hard to avoid. She pierced me with her hypnotizing eyes, a look of pure betrayal staring back at me, and it felt like someone had reached in and ripped my heart out.

I'd never felt so ashamed of myself, and I'd done a lot of shady things. But that look made me regret not coming clean with her sooner. Maybe then I could've had a chance with her instead of the scraps I'd been relegated to devour.

Despite her cold shoulder, I couldn't seem to

leave, and I found any excuse I could to stay in Utah. First, it had been to help the Agency take down the Council. Then was the job offer from Samson to work with him at Alpha Security Solutions. I took a hiatus from my post, so I could be near a girl who didn't even like to be in the same room as me.

So when she disappeared, I knew it was time to quit staying in the shadows, hoping she'd recognize me and forgive my transgression. Sawyer had sat me down at one point and told me that the fastest way into Finley's heart was to be honest, but I couldn't even seem to be honest with myself.

Facing her departure, I knew it was time. Time to correct the one regret I had in my life.

So, I used all my resources, and I tracked her down and went to Asa, knowing I needed to figure out a way to make it work. If Fin wouldn't give me a chance, at least I could bring them back together. I owed her that. Asa was a good guy and someone she deserved. He'd surprised me when he asked my feelings about his girlfriend, and for a second, I'd hoped before remembering the crushing reality of my life. I didn't get the girl.

"What do you mean?" I asked, shuffling my feet. "I care for her. She's a good friend."

"Listen, I know I haven't been the most open,

avoiding the fact that my girlfriend seems to collect men like they're lost puppies. I can't say I know what she feels, but she's worked hard at ignoring you, and the other guy we don't mention, too hard for it just to be friendship."

"Milo?" I asked, raising my brow, purposefully ignoring the part about me.

"Yeah, but since you're here, let's talk about you."

Sighing, I nodded, dropping my arms. "I met Fin when she was seventeen, both online and in person. I didn't know they were the same girl for a while. I had a crush on her, it's hard not to. But that's not in the cards for us. I'm here to make sure she's safe and to help you get her back. She deserves to be happy."

Asa watched me for a while before walking over. He dumped his empty plates into the sink and turned to look at me. "I didn't know how I'd feel thinking about my girlfriend with someone else, but I can't deny that it's nice having you here. You're a good guy despite your outward appearance. I won't stand in the way if Fin decides she wants to give you a chance. I've experienced life with and without her now, and I much prefer the one with her. Even if that means sharing her, I'm cool with that. We can figure something out together."

"Yeah, well, let's just focus on finding her first."

I knew the reality of this and told myself the plan

was to let her go, to let them be together. But when she walked into that hotel room looking like a drowned rat, I couldn't seem to catch my breath.

I was only kidding myself if I thought I could let her go without a fight again. Asa had said he wanted to figure something out, so maybe I should take him up on that conversation for once.

"I wondered when you would show up."

Sitting forward, I rubbed my sweaty palms on the knees of my jeans. I looked her over, assessing for any sign of injury. It didn't appear she was hurt, just covered in some substance and she'd never looked cuter. I pushed aside the urge to go to her and wrap her in my arms. I hadn't earned that privilege yet.

"You didn't make it easy."

She snorted, reaching into a bag to pull out some clothes and sniffed them. She cursed, holding up a pair of stretchy pants and a tank top, and I assumed they were dirty. She sighed, sitting on the edge of the bed, looking at me.

"I've had a shitty night, and I haven't had time to do laundry, and now I'm out of clothes. So, can we possibly move this interrogation to the laundromat, or even better, wait until morning?"

I was tempted to let her have the time, but I knew if I did, she'd somehow manage to escape me, and it would be another month before I found her.

"No can do, sweetheart. I'll do you one better. Go take a shower, and I'll have something for you." She eyed me, her gaze calculating as she tried to figure out my angle.

"I'm too tired to care. Fine. Don't touch anything."

I snorted, like that would stop me. I'd already gone through all of her things anyway. Nothing for me to find now. I didn't even regret placing a tracker on her laptop while I waited. It would be interesting to see how long she took to find it.

She grabbed the few things she had and went into the bathroom. As soon as the door was shut, I pulled out my phone, needing to send a few messages.

ME: She's here and in need of some clothes. You got it or want me to send out for something?

ASA: I'll take care of it. Does she know I'm here?

ME: Not yet. How far out are you?

ASA: I'm in the lobby. I'll go grab some things and be right up.

ME: She's in the shower now

ASA: Okay, thanks, Cohen.

I sent the other two I needed to send with that out of the way.

ME: Located the target. In possession. Will update you on progress.
Samson: Good job. I'll update the others.

ME: Contact made.
Superior: Good. Be discreet.

I snorted at that. I didn't think we had the same definitions of the word, but I'd be as discreet as possible. The water shut off, and I put my phone away, wondering if she was one of those girls who would take an hour after she got out or be out here in five minutes. With Finley, I never could tell. She was high maintenance without always being high maintenance, leaving me confused about what to expect from her most of the time.

A knock at the door had me standing, so I walked over and peeked out, finding Asa standing with a shopping bag. Letting him in, I took the bag and knocked on the bathroom door while he slipped behind me so she wouldn't see him yet.

"Fin. I got your clothes."

The door opened a crack, and her hand reached out. I placed the bag into her grip, and she pulled it back, closing the door. I went back to the chair I'd been sitting in and sat back down, nodding to Asa as he stood by the wall. He looked nervous, and I didn't blame him. She'd been somewhat receptive to me so far, but I wasn't sure how she would react to him.

When the door opened a few seconds later, she stepped out in new clothes and a towel on her head. She narrowed her eyes at me, her arms crossed.

"I don't know if I should be impressed you knew my sizes or weirded out. I'm beginning to think you're some kind of stalker, Chaos."

"It's Cohen. I only go by that online. You know how it is." I shrugged, wanting her to see me as a person outside of my hacker identity. It was the first time I'd wanted that, and it felt important.

"As for the clothes, I didn't get them. He did." I nodded to the corner Asa stood in. At my motion, her head swiveled, the towel swinging with the movement. I heard her gasp, and her body moved a step before she stopped herself.

"Asa," she said, her voice soft and unsure.

Apparently, it was all he needed, and he took the rest of the steps between them, pulling her into his arms. I should've given them a moment, but I was greedy, and I sucked up their reunion like an emotional parasite, pretending it was for me.

Finley clung to him in a way no one had ever

touched me, and I envied their relationship. If I was more selfless, I'd let her go and let them have their love story. But I wasn't. I'd been kidding myself earlier.

I was greedy and lived my life taking what I wanted, and I knew now this was something I couldn't walk away from. I never pictured myself as part of a poly relationship, but if it got me a chance with the girl of my dreams, then I'd try it. Besides, I wasn't one for convention anyway, bucking tradition with everything else I did in my life.

I cleared my throat when the emotions became too much, and Asa looked up, meeting my eyes. His gaze held something I didn't want to think about, his assessment of me too on point for my liking.

"Fin, I know you wanted to do this independently, but I couldn't just stand by. I tried, I really did, but I was miserable. So, I'm being selfish and asking you to let me stay. Let us help," he pleaded as she clung to him.

Her shoulders sagged as she turned, taking a step away from his embrace. She looked between the two of us, and I could already see the rejection on her face. I'd gotten used to that look from her. So, I stepped in, hoping I could use my powers for good.

"I know who you're trying to find, and you won't. Not without my help."

Her retort died on her lips as she huffed, crossing her arms. I lifted an eyebrow, waiting her out. She knew it was true, even if she didn't want to acknowledge it. I leaned forward, my elbows on my knees as I watched her, not breaking eye contact.

"Give us a chance, Fin," Asa begged, reaching out to touch her. She didn't shake him off, and I knew she was close to submitting.

"How about we broker a trade?" I asked, sitting back and placing my leg over my knee. I knew how Fin operated by this point in our friendship. She didn't like to be a burden and would be more likely to give in if it was a trade.

"What kind of trade?"

The corner of my mouth tilted up, and I moved my hand to cover it. "Well, it would do me a huge favor to have your boyfriend off my back about finding you, first off. He's been such a chatty fellow, so I could really use the quiet time to get some actual work done." Asa snorted, but let me continue.

"That doesn't seem like much of a trade, to be honest. No offense, honey," she said, blushing up at Asa.

"Okay, fine." I blew out a breath, debating how much to reveal. They told me to be discreet, but I was learning that didn't really work with Fin. "Let us help, and I'll give you access to my computer for one hour. Anything you can find program-wise, you can copy. That's it. My final offer."

Her eyes went huge, and she licked her lips. Accessing another hacker's system with free rein was the ultimate gift. I was taking a gamble she wouldn't find anything too incriminating about what I did in my spare time. It felt worth it to win the chance to do this with her. No matter the cost.

"Deal." She stuck her hand out, and I stood, taking it. I pulled her closer, rubbing my thumb over the backside of her hand.

"You can't get rid of me now, sweetheart."

I could've sworn I saw her gulp, her eyes dilating at the message, but it flicked away so quickly, that I couldn't be sure.

"So, what have you learned so far?" I asked as she sat on the bed, Asa next to her. I leaned against the dresser, cutting the distance between us. This was my last chance to win over Finley Reyes, and I would make sure she couldn't ignore me.

COHEN PEERED at me with such an unrelenting gaze I didn't know how to handle it. Over the past few months, he'd constantly been there, waiting for me to say something. But I never did. The fear of wanting too much, of being scared to take more than I was given, held me back.

That and I didn't know how to trust him.

While he hadn't betrayed me in the way that Blackhawk had, it still stung to know he'd known who I was and hadn't told me. Years of friendship, and he kept that from me. It made me feel like he was keeping something else hidden.

And that hit too close to home for me to examine. Better to push him aside, so I didn't have to look at my own flaws.

Asa's hand picked up mine, and I gave up the fight of trying to push him away. Asa always had a knack for making me putty in his hands. He was too good, but I was too weak at the moment after weeks of no contact to deny myself any longer.

That small amount of contact gave me the strength to answer Cohen's stare.

"Not as much as I'd like. I found Blackhawk and he reached out, saying he had a job for me. He sent me to this town."

"Blackhawk?" Asa asked, pulling my attention.

"When I was first looking for your sister, I taught myself to code and took a few classes. I needed information that I couldn't get from legal sources, so I asked around and discovered a club, The MidKnight Guild. Being part of MKG would've granted me access to databases, programs, and keys to almost anything. In order to be part of it, you have to prove your skills. They match you up with other hackers, and as a team, you're given tasks. They varied in skill and difficulty. There were four of us at first, but by the end, it was just Obsidian and Blackhawk. I thought we were friends..." I shook my head, fighting back the tears that wanted to fall.

"I'd met Blackhawk through another club, and he sent me Oblivion's information. I was, um," Cohen cleared his throat, the first sign of remorse I'd ever seen from him as he spoke. "I'd just gotten a summer internship with Fin's dad. I didn't know she was Oblivion until afterward when I heard the news of her arrest. I didn't want to believe that the badass hacker chick was the seventeen-year-old daughter of my boss."

He paused, stepping forward and squatting so he was at eye level. Cohen picked up my free hand, his thumb rubbing across it in a way that felt too natural.

"I'm sorry I never told you afterward that I knew you. That wasn't cool of me. At first, I didn't want to blur lines. But after a while, it felt too late to say anything. The dread weighed on me that you wouldn't hear me out if you ever found out. I'd just be the weirdo who kept this huge secret from you. I'm sorry for that. It wasn't fair. And I hope you know that it's the one thing in my life I regret. Your friendship meant something to me, and I should've been brave enough to tell you the truth."

I searched his eyes, realizing how blue they were this close. They always seemed so stormy far away, but not at this moment; they were as clear as a sunny day.

"You're forgiven, and honestly, I wasn't too upset when I found out. That night was a lot to deal with, so it was easier to pretend it was because of you. I've been cowardly not saying anything either when we've worked together, so I'm sorry."

He smiled, and I couldn't deny how it made my insides flip. Even when I thought he was just my dad's dorky intern, he always had. I was just too lost in my own world to notice back then.

"Just to clear the air," Asa started, clearing his throat.

Looking at him, I was worried I'd see the disgust on his face after I stared into another guy's eyes, but I didn't. Asa proved to me again how good he was and how much I didn't deserve him. He looked at me with nothing but love and understanding.

"Cohen and I talked a lot these past weeks, and I've gotten to know him. Whatever you two feel for each other or don't feel for each other, that's for you to decide. Don't let me stand in the way of that."

"Wait!" I shouted, grabbing his hand firmly as fear started to engulf me. "Are you saying you're walking away?" Tears I'd been holding back for weeks came to the surface, and I felt like I was on a precipice as I waited for him to answer. Asa screwed up his nose, and I couldn't take it any longer as words began to flow out of my mouth.

"Asa, no, please don't do this. I'm sorry. I thought

I had to leave, that we were strong enough. I don't want to lose you. I can't. I love you." I threw my arms around his neck as I sobbed, deciding I'd find a way to hold him hostage or something until he loved me again.

"Fin," he soothed, "Fin, no, it's not that. Shh, don't cry." He rocked me back and forth, his hand rubbing up my back. The towel I had wrapped around my head had gone askew from the movement, and my wet hair began to fall out of it. I couldn't make out words as he tried to comfort me, too consumed by my own fear.

I felt the towel be moved off my head, releasing a lot of pressure. It took a while for me to realize that someone was combing it out as well, the gentle strokes soothing me even more. When I finally was able to stop my tears, I could hear what Asa was saying.

"I love you, Finley. I'm not walking away. I'm just saying you don't have to just choose me. I don't want to live my life without you. You're my everything. I've been so lost without you these past few weeks. I promise I'm not leaving. I just want to be with you. Always."

I sat back, wiping my face, looking at him. His green eyes sparkled, and I realized it was because of the tears he'd shed as well. I cupped his face, kissing his lips briefly. I hadn't let myself do that earlier, too afraid of the answer. But now, it felt like the most natural thing, and I knew we both needed it.

When I leaned back, I felt another body behind me. I tensed for a second but then relaxed, knowing it was Cohen and he'd been the one to brush my hair. Leaning my head against him, I tilted it up and found him peering down at me.

"Thank you, that felt nice."

"Anytime, sweetheart. Especially if I get to be part of the activity that makes you wet, to begin with." He winked at me, and I froze, not sure how to take the flirting. When I heard Asa chuckle, it released the tension in me, and I let out my own giggle.

"I will have to get used to you flirting with me, aren't I?"

"It's my love language." He grinned, and I had a feeling I'd come to crave those smiles if I let myself.

Sitting up, I turned so I could look at both of them. "I'm not sure where my heart is right now. I've denied it for so long; I think it's default is to hide away from me. I know that there are times I feel like my insides might explode when I'm around you, but it's hard for me to reconcile that. I've never been the girl that guys wanted. I was the nerdy, weird girl in school and then once I got in trouble, only the guys who thought that meant I was easy were interested. Before Asa, I'd only had sex twice, and it hadn't been pleasant. I'm scared that if I let myself want more, that it will be taken away from me."

Asa squeezed my hand, kissing it. "I'm not going anywhere, and maybe you just need to let yourself be open to the idea instead of putting pressure on yourself to know now."

"I'm not expecting you to just start making out with me, you know. There needs to be foreplay," Cohen said, chuckling before his face turned serious. "For now, I'm just making my intentions known so that there's no miscommunication. Maybe we should get back to why we're here and leave the matters of the heart for another day?"

"Right, yes, perfect." I nodded my head a little too aggressively, my hair swinging back and forth as the wet strands hit my cheeks.

"So you were telling us about Blackhawk," Asa prompted, giving me my out.

"Yes, I thought we were friends. But on the last mission, I was set up and arrested. It wasn't my first time. I'd gotten into a few other things over the year but always let off. This... it was more serious. I was charged, and after a night in juvy, I was given 300 hours of community service. It left a bitter taste in my mouth, especially when I got my computer back and found I'd been kicked off the server and ghosted by my two supposed friends."

I took a breath, the anger and rage coursing through me again.

"So, you're what, after revenge? And why just Blackhawk and not Obsidian?" Asa asked.

"Because Blackhawk and I had a relationship outside of our team. Obsidian wasn't part of that. He was a bit of a control freak, but he was sweet overall. No, it was Blackhawk. He was the one who told me to meet him, and then he never showed, but the police did."

"How much of a relationship?" Asa asked.

I sighed, blowing out a breath. "He was the first guy I thought I loved. I was only seventeen, and he fought his attraction to me, but eventually, things between us became more. He sent me gifts and was the one person I felt saw me during that time. It was a dark period of my life, and he saved me in many ways. His betrayal hurt, but I also realized how far down the dark side I'd gone. He'd set me up to take the fall, and the things I did, I hate myself for them. Until I deal with him, I don't feel like I deserve a future. He stole some of my innocence, and I will never get it back. But maybe I can stop him from hurting others. I don't really know why it's so important, but after I was taken, it was like, all I could think about was the first reckless mistake I made, and how maybe if I corrected it, then I'd be okay, I'd have a chance at a future without feeling so broken."

Tears threatened to come again, and I realized how much I'd just spilled to them. More than I'd admitted to even myself. Purging it from my chest felt good, though, and it helped remind me of my purpose.

"You think revenge is the best course?" Cohen asked.

"It's the only way I think I can get that part of me that was broken that night, by making him pay."

"Okay, I'll help. It's not going to be easy."

"Thank you. I appreciate it." I turned to Asa, needing to know his response. "You?"

He bit his lip, looking me over. "If this is what you need, I'll help however I can."

I kissed his cheek, squeezing his hand. "I love you, Asa."

He softened, kissing my temple as he pulled me into his arms. I looked over at Cohen as he watched us. I didn't know what I expected to see, but it wasn't lust. Swallowing, I dropped my eyes, not ready to examine that yet.

"Once I got here, Blackhawk sent me to do surveillance on a building and then wait for his contact in a cowboy hat. It turned out, it was him, but I didn't know that until I got back to the hotel room and opened the envelope. In the process of searching for him, I was doused with a tray of drinks, and it ruined my computer. I had to call Milo to get a new one."

"Milo? Is he here?" Asa asked.

I shook my head. "No, he's just been helping me."

"The one person we didn't think to ask," Cohen said, smiling. "You're smart, Finley Reyes. So, what happened after that?"

Getting up, I grabbed the paper and handed it to Cohen. "Apparently, there wasn't a job, but another puzzle to find him. By the time I got to the location, I was too late and was doused in paint. Though," I said, snapping my fingers and pulling out the piece of register tape from my pocket. "There was a message in morse code. We just need to decode it."

Cohen's eyes lit up, reaching for it, but stopped himself. "May I?"

Nodding, he took it, and an excited look came across his face as he went back to the table and pulled out his laptop.

I sat back on the bed, taking Asa's hand. "I am

glad you're here. I'm sorry for running away. I thought it was the best option at the time."

"I know, Fin. I'm here now." He kissed me, pulling me into a hug. "You have to be the one to tell Sawyer, though."

Cringing, I knew he was right as a laugh bubbled out of me. "Fine."

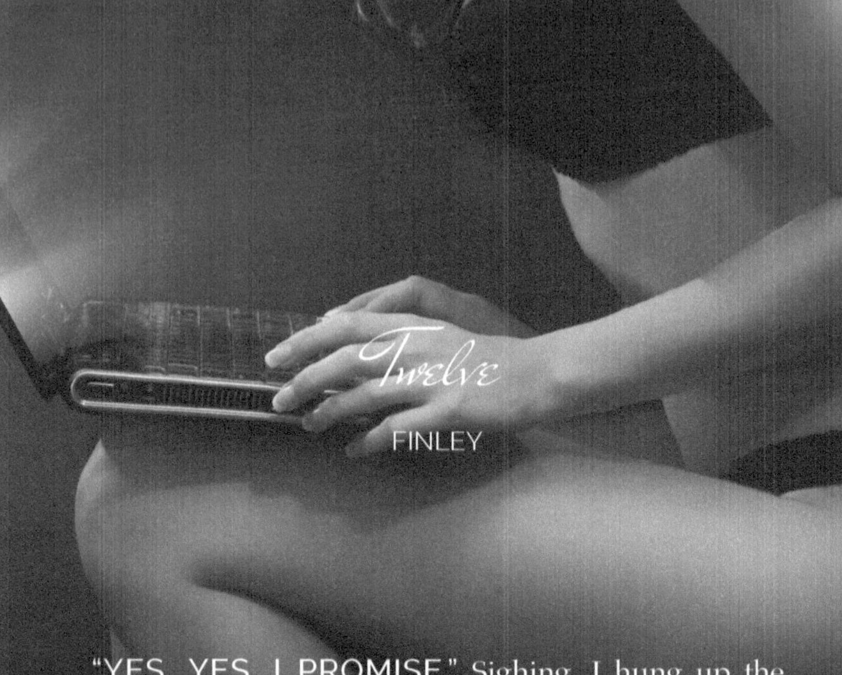

Twelve

FINLEY

"YES, YES, I PROMISE." Sighing, I hung up the phone and stayed against the wall for a moment. I'd stepped out into the hallway for some privacy since I knew Sawyer would yell, and she had, but then there had been a lot of tears and talking through things that had been needed.

It was sad to say that it had taken me this long to realize I was stubborn and didn't like to let people help me. Shocker, I know.

Feeling lighter now that I wasn't hiding from everyone, I inserted the keycard and stepped back into the room. Asa and Cohen were bent over his computer as they worked on the morse code riddle at the table. It had taken Cohen no time to crack it; apparently, he was fluent in morse code. But the message hadn't made sense.

I can crawl, I can fly, I have hands but no legs or wings either. What am I? Have you forgotten?

Asa looked up when the door clicked, meeting my eyes. It felt nicer having him here, not doing this alone. I needed to remember that for the future and stop running off by myself.

"How'd she take it?" he asked, coming closer.

"There was a lot of yelling and then crying, but I feel better. I promised her I'd stay with you and wouldn't try to leave you guys once you fell asleep."

"Shit, I hadn't even thought of that." His face whitened, and I felt even worse for the pain I'd caused him.

"Yeah, well, I wouldn't say I hadn't thought about it, and Sawyer knew me well enough to call me out on it. But, I realized how lonely I was and out of my depth. I need you guys for my own sanity. I'd started talking to myself for the company, which isn't a fun place to be." I cringed, my cheeks blushing.

"Oh, to be a fly on the wall for those conversations." Asa chuckled, making me feel better. He always had a knack for doing that.

"You guys make any progress?" I asked, a yawn following it.

"A little bit, but it can wait until morning. Come on, let's get some rest."

It was on the tip of my tongue to argue, but I

could see the dark circles under his eyes. Asa and Cohen had said how they'd followed my trail together for a while, but at the last stop, they split up, not knowing which direction was the right one. When Cohen found me, Asa turned around and met him here. They'd both been up for almost twenty hours at this point.

"Okay, that sounds great."

"Cohen, you going to keep working?" I asked, leading Asa to the bed. There was only one in the room since it had just been me. He peered up, looking at us. It took him a second to realize I had asked something.

"Oh yeah, I'll catch some sleep in a bit. Don't worry about me." He yawned, and I saw the dark circles under his eyes too.

"Nope," I decided, dropping Asa's hand to walk over to the table. I shut the laptop and grabbed his hand. He didn't make it easy as I tried to pull his big frame up from the chair. "You could help, turd."

"Turd? Ah, you do like me," he teased.

Rolling my eyes, I kept pulling, and he finally gave in and stood. Asa had already crawled into the bed on one side, and I realized what it meant. Me between them. Okay, girl, you could do this. It wasn't a big deal.

Swallowing, I turned off the main light and

crawled into the bed, letting Asa wrap his arms around me. Cohen hesitated for a second, looking at us.

"Come on, turd. You need sleep. We can be adults and share a bed."

He nodded, debating something. Eventually, he kicked off his shoes and began to unbutton his jeans.

"Um, what are you doing?" I screeched, covering my eyes. I could feel Asa's chest rumbling behind me.

"It's fine, Fin. He's just taking off his jeans. They're not the most comfortable thing to sleep in."

"Oh, yeah," I said, realizing how I'd jumped to conclusions too fast. My cheeks flamed, and when I dropped my hand, I found Cohen smirking at me. He slipped under the covers and turned off the lamp on the table. It was quiet as we all settled, our own thoughts running through our heads.

As the breathing evened out, I fell asleep quickly, for the first time in a while, if I was honest. I didn't have to be on guard now. I had people with me who would help take watch. It was nice, and I fell into a deep sleep and didn't wake again until morning.

WHISPERING WOKE me the following day, and when I stretched, I noticed that the bed was empty. Something about that had me pouting as I opened my eyes. When I looked around for the guys, they were grinning at me.

"What?" I asked, wiping my face for any drool.

"You're cute when you sleep," Cohen said, looking at me in a way I wasn't used to.

"Here," Asa said, picking up a bag and cup off the table. I eagerly sat up, pushing the covers down when I saw what it was.

"Ah, you do love me," I beamed as Asa handed me the cup of coffee.

"I do." He smiled lovingly, making me realize how dumb I was. "But Cohen was the one to get the food and coffee."

"Oh," I said, my fingers around the coffee as I inhaled it. "Thanks, Cohen." I looked up at him from under my eyelashes and found him blushing. It was such an odd look on his usually cocky face that I did a double-take. "Are you blushing?" I teased.

He scoffed, waving me off as he focused on the computer. "Nope. I don't even know what that is."

Laughing, I took the chocolate croissant that Asa held out and immediately shoved it into my mouth. A moan escaped me as the chocolate and flaky pastry melted in my mouth. "That's so good."

When I finished licking my fingers, I looked up to find both guys watching me with hungry looks. I was used to seeing it from Asa, but it still surprised me to find it reflected back in Cohen's eyes.

"Sorry. I was hungry."

"Never apologize for enjoying something, sweetheart," Cohen said, his voice a little soft. "I, um, I think I figured out the clue."

My eyes went wide, and I scooted off the bed so I could look at the screen. Cohen didn't move when I approached, my body brushing against his arm as I leaned closer to inspect what he had. Turning my head, I found him watching me.

"Am I in the way?" I asked. I think I heard Asa snort behind me, but I didn't dare look away from Cohen.

"Nope. In fact, you have a seat right here." Before I could protest, he pulled me down into his lap, locking me in with his arms around my waist. Resting his head on my shoulder, I heard him sigh.

"So, I realized that he was using a quote from a book—*Forgotten Time*."

"Huh, that kind of makes sense." Memories of us discussing it began to emerge, and I shut them down, not wanting to fall into the past when I was with them.

"Based on that, I think his next location will be the theme park."

"It's real?" I asked, not realizing it had been about an actual place.

"I don't know if it's the one from the book, but there is one named Raven Time. I think he'll be at the funhouse."

"How do you know that?" I asked, turning my head, forgetting I was sitting on his lap, bringing our faces dangerously close.

He swallowed, his eyes bouncing back and forth from my lips to my eyes. "Because after the quote was the following. 'The fun begins on Tuesday at 7:00 pm.' So, my guess is he's telling you when and where. You just had to figure out the where first."

"You're brilliant, you know?" I smiled, happiness fluttering through me. I never would've solved that in time.

Cohen's cheeks did that thing he denied and reddened, causing me to smirk. I liked how I was affecting him.

"How long does it take to get there from here?" Asa asked.

I grabbed the phone and put it on the map, and he hovered over my other shoulder as it calculated. "Looks like about eight hours," I sighed.

"Looks like we're going on a road trip then," Asa

beamed down at me. I grinned back, not hating the idea with him along.

"You make everything better. I was stupid to think I could do this without you," I admitted. Reaching up, I pulled his face down to mine, kissing him.

"If you're going to be handing out kisses, my lips are right here," Cohen said into my ear, his lips brushing against my neck in the process. Tiny tingles shot through me and goosebumps appeared on my arms at the slight touch. I sucked in a breath, and I could've sworn I heard him growl in my ear as he shifted beneath me.

"Shit, I have no clothes," I said, remembering I needed to do laundry as I tried to distract myself from rubbing my butt into the hard length I felt growing beneath me.

"We can buy you some things for now and do it once we're there," Asa offered.

"Or you just go naked," Cohen stated, no longer trying to hide how aroused he was from me sitting on his lap.

Swallowing, I tried to focus on the computer screen. "Clothes, yeah, good idea."

Cohen chuckled darkly behind me, the air fanning against my neck, doing nothing to help with my current state.

"Do you need to take a shower?" Asa asked, a hint of amusement in his voice. "I can go grab you some more things if you do."

"Shower, um, no, not really. I'm good for now. I guess we can pack up then and head out. Do you guys have a car? I hopped between a rental and the bus."

"Yeah, I have a car," Cohen said, not releasing me. I kept tapping his arm, hoping he'd get the message. My self-control to not rub my butt into his cock was lessening the longer I sat there.

"Perfect. It's settled then."

He still didn't let me go, and I looked up to find Asa, smirking. "I'll be back in a few minutes then. Don't kill each other."

With that, my boyfriend left me practically panting on another guy's lap as he strolled out like he didn't care. Rude.

"Um, can I get up, please?" I asked, deciding to try going for the direct approach.

"Nope," he said, doubling down and pulling me closer. "I kind of like having you here where you can't get away."

"Okay, cool, but I can't live here."

"Why not?" he asked, and I could hear the smile in his voice.

"Well, as nice as it is, I need to pee and do other

things at times. And it would get awfully sweaty after a while, I bet."

"I'm hoping it gets sweaty, sweetheart. That means it's good."

Gulping, I nodded, trying to find words. "Well, okay, good, um, but still."

He laughed, his breath cascading over my neck again. "Fine. I'll let you up. This is my new favorite thing, though. I should've told you who I was years ago. Be prepared for more of this. Once I latch on, I don't really let go."

The barest of kisses was placed under my ear. His lips were warm, only giving the slightest pressure, but it was enough to send a ping straight to my core, making it throb as my toes curled under.

"I honestly don't think I would've been ready for you back then," I admitted, standing up once his arms released me.

When I stood to turn, his hand reached out, taking mine. "I'm glad we have now."

It was the simplest phrase, but it resonated with me. "Me too, Cohen."

I found myself smiling as I stepped out from between his legs and began to pack up the few meager belongings I had scattered around the room. Asa was back in a few, and I changed in the bathroom. I realized they'd also changed clothes, small bags sitting next to mine when I returned. It felt odd to be leaving with them, but I liked it more than having to sneak out on my own.

"Alright, let's hit the road."

FINLEY, AGE 17

Blackhawk: You kind of remind me of the heroine from the book, Forgotten Time. Have you ever read it?

Oblivion: Are you joking with me right now?

Blackhawk: No. I read. I'm kind of offended you think I can't read.

Oblivion: No, that's not it. Sorry. It's just… that's one of my favorite books. I've read it a million times probably. It's kind of surreal that a guy is telling me I remind them of Raven. She's kind of a badass.

Blackhawk: So are you, little hacker.

Oblivion: It doesn't feel that way in real life.

Blackhawk: You'll find your friend. I believe in you. Did you message Chaos?

Oblivion: Yes. He's looking into some things.

Blackhawk: That sounds promising.

Oblivion: Yeah, I guess. Her birthday was yesterday and it just feels weird not cele-brating with her. That's two I've missed now.

Blackhawk: Time is a construct. When you're reunited, it won't feel like any has passed.

Oblivion: Yeah, I hope so. It feels like it's too much to wish for.

Blackhawk: You deserve all the things, little hacker. In fact, I want to send you something.

Oblivion: Isn't that against the rules. No personal information.

Blackhawk: Which is why I have an idea. Have you ever heard of a virtual address?

Oblivion: No, what is it?

Blackhawk: There are some sites where you can have a virtual address and use it to avoid huge shipping fees on things for international. Then once you've accumulated a certain amount in your storage container, it's shipped to you all at once. How about we both sign up for one and it keeps us still in the spirit of the program?

Oblivion: Um, sure.

Blackhawk: Until then, little hacker. We always have Raven.

THE FIRST HOUR had been quiet as we settled into the drive, listening to the GPS navigate us out of the city. The early morning combined with the last few days caught up with me, and my head leaned against the window as my eyes drew heavy.

I'd fallen into that weird conscious, but unconscious state, where I knew I was asleep, but I wasn't dead to the world. So when the dream started, it felt like I was watching it play out like a movie, reliving the past, but I was unable to stop it or make any different choices.

"What is this place?" I asked as I managed to crawl through a window into the basement. I tumbled into a few boxes as I landed and I quickly jumped up to see if anyone had heard me.

"It's an abandoned house. Does it matter?" Obsidian

said through my earbud. I'd remembered to bring them this time, meaning I didn't have to have it on speaker. Which was good when I was meant to be stealthy.

"I guess not. It's just kind of an odd request."

"I thought that too," Blackhawk started, but was cut off by Obsidian.

"Listen, as team leader, I pick from the pool of tasks I think we can do and which will give us the best opportunity to make it."

"Yeah, yeah," I grumbled, brushing off the dust I'd collected on me. "Why am I the only one who breaks into places?"

"Because you're the best at it."

"Flattery will get you nowhere," I teased, but secretly liking that Blackhawk noticed my skills.

"With us being only three members now, we have to make a splash," Obsidian continued, ignoring the flirting. He'd gotten pretty good at doing that.

"Ugh, don't remind me. I can't believe Mongoose bailed on us." Sighing, I pulled out the mini flashlight and looked around the room. "I don't see anything other than boxes. What should I take to show we were here?"

"Are there any files, or I don't know brochures? Just something with a logo on it."

"Sure, let me pull up the mystery place's Wikipedia and see what's in each box," I sassed, rolling my eyes.

A deep chuckle came across the app, and even distorted,

I knew it was Blackhawk's. Spotting a box that said office, I walked over to it and began to open it. Thankfully, there was a brochure on top, so I plucked it and hoped it was for this place. Smoothing it out, I shined the light onto it.

"Magnolia House," I murmured. "Found something. Okay, I'm getting out of here."

"Grab a file too. I'm curious," Obsidian said. Sighing, I grabbed a couple of folders off the top and shoved them down the back of my pants, pulling my shirt over them.

"Got it. Now, I'm leaving. This place gives me the creeps and it stinks."

"Be careful, little hacker. We need you on our team."

Smiling, I climbed out the window and closed it as I dashed off toward the street I'd parked on. Pulling my disguise off, I went to sign out of the app when I noticed a message in my inbox. Clicking on it, I was surprised by who it was from.

Mongoose: Oblivion, I need your help. Can we talk?

JERKING UP, it took a few moments for me to realize we were still in the car. Peering around, I found Cohen still driving. He peeked over at me, a concerned look on his face.

"You okay, sweetheart?"

Wiping my mouth, I nodded, trying to rid myself of the dream. It felt like I'd been right back there.

"Yeah, just a weird dream."

He reached over and squeezed my leg, giving me some comfort. I looked back and found Asa had his eyes closed on the seat, so I turned back to the front. Music played softly as we drove, and thoughts I'd been trying to ignore about the two men in the car began to filter through. It was like my brain was going to make me think about one thing or the other. I couldn't ignore both.

The guys seemed to have accepted what I'd shared with them about my past and why I'd left, but would they when I told them everything?

Was I only asking for heartache getting involved with Cohen, too? I think I had it best when I just focused on one boy. Less likely to screw it up that way.

Twisting my body to get comfortable, I jumped when a hand clamped down on my thigh. I followed the arm up to find it belonged to Cohen.

"Stop whatever torture you're putting yourself through right now. Quit trying to predict everything and just let things happen."

"I—"

"You were. You forget that we both know you,"

Asa piped in from the back, apparently not as asleep as I'd assumed. He leaned forward, poking his head between the seats. "Trust, babe."

"How did you know?" I asked, noticing that Cohen wasn't in any hurry to move his hand.

"You've moved every two seconds and have sighed or huffed every three."

Chuckling, I tried not to think about how hot my face was getting. "Sorry." I turned my head to look out the window, needing a little space. Asa had insisted on letting me sit up here, but it felt like I was under a spotlight.

"How about we play a game to get to know one another better?" Asa asked, pulling me back to face him.

"What kind of game?" The mention of games had me souring, the ones with Blackhawk not ending how I ever thought they would.

"Since we're in a car, we could do something like 20 Questions or two truths and a lie."

"Two truths and a lie?" I asked, not having heard of it before.

"It's exactly as it sounds. You give two truths and one lie, and we have to try to figure out which one is the lie."

"Huh, okay, that sounds interesting. You first, though," I teased, giving him a peck on the lips.

Asa smiled brightly, warming my insides. I swear, he had the power to light the whole world, or at least mine.

"You in, Cohen?" Asa asked.

"Yeah, sure, why not." He shrugged, and I realized his thumb had started to rub on the inside of my leg. Swallowing, I debated moving so it would make his hand move, but I hadn't found the willpower yet to do it.

"Hmm, okay. I've got it. I once met Hulk Hogan. I'm allergic to strawberries. I've never roller skated." He ticked them off on his fingers, saying them all with the same tone of voice, giving nothing away. It had me looking at my boyfriend in a whole new way. I observed his facial features as he stared at me, grinning.

"Hmm." I tapped my finger on my lips as I debated.

"I know," Cohen said smugly. "You guess first, sweetheart."

My cheeks warmed, and I didn't know if I hated or loved when he called me that. "Fine, turd." I stuck out my tongue, again trying to take their attention away from my ever-heating cheeks.

"Geesh, I feel like a horrible girlfriend. I'm going to go with Hulk Hogan." I sat back, looking over at Cohen. He still had his smug face as he navigated around a car, turning his blinker on. He had to move his hand to grab the wheel, and I hated how much I missed it already.

"Nope, it's roller skating," he answered, peering into the rearview mirror. His smug smile grew at whatever he saw there, and I whipped my head around to look at Asa.

"He's right?" I asked a slight screech to my voice.

"Yup," Asa said, laughing.

"But... but..." I sputtered, not understanding. "You've met Hulk Hogan? I knew about the strawberries, thank God, or I'd be a worthless girlfriend."

"Hey," Asa said, grabbing my face, stopping me from spiraling. "It's a game to get to know one another. I picked things I knew you wouldn't know. It's not meant to make you feel bad." His palms cupped my whole face, the rough sides of his hands feeling comforting as he stared into my eyes. Eventually, I nodded, licking my lips.

"Okay. You're right. Will you tell me about it?"

He smiled, leaning forward to press his lips softly against mine. "I'd love to." He sat back and told Cohen and me about the time he was at laser tag with his school friends and ran into Hulk Hogan, who was there for a birthday party for his son.

"He was really cool. He took a picture with us and everything. I thought I was the optimum of cool for years, and then no one knew who he was, and it no longer mattered." We all laughed, the sound filling the car. "You're up, Cohen, since you guessed right. How'd you know?"

"I'm not giving my secret away, dude." He smirked, glancing up at the mirror again. "And I've got the perfect three. You guys ready?"

We nodded, and I leaned forward, turning in my seat with my leg bent as I peered at the two guys. I wasn't trying to bring my body closer, so he'd touch me again. Nope, not at all.

"I was once stood up because I was too edgy. I have a sister I've never met. I'm a millionaire."

I thought over the things he said, trying to hear them how he told them to see if he'd gone up any on certain words. But like Asa, I couldn't tell any of them from the other. Deciding to go with the most far-fetched, I glanced up, finding he was looking at me out of the corner of his eye.

"What do you think, Fin?"

"Millionaire is a lie."

He didn't say anything, looking at Asa to give his response. "Your guess, man?"

"Sister." Asa nodded like he was trying to sound more sure of the answer himself.

"I'm hurt, you guys," Cohen said. "To think you

both believe I've been stood up! Obviously, I need to up my game if you both assume that to be true."

"Wait... so you are a millionaire?" I asked, gasping.

He turned his head to glance at me quickly before focusing on the road. "Um, yeah. I was a genius hacker, remember? What did you think I was doing?"

"But... I guess..." My brain stopped. "You kept the money? It made me feel dirty, and after everything went down, I used it to repay for some of the damage I caused." I swallowed, not wanting to go into details yet. I wasn't ready to face that dark secret.

"In the beginning, I wasn't on the right side of things. I got caught once, too, you know. When I was twelve, I hacked into an organization, and they caught me. Instead of pressing charges, they gave me a job."

"At twelve? I feel like I don't really know you," I admitted.

"Yes, at twelve. They gave me training, a home, really."

"So, when we met, when you worked for my dad, you were what... undercover? Isn't that illegal? Corporate Espionage?"

"Whoa there, firecracker. You're jumping to conclusions. I did things off and on and lived my life as I wanted in the meantime. School and working as an intern were all part of my training for my masters."

"You have a master's? Why…" I shook my head. "I don't really know you."

"I actually have my doctorate now," he said sheepishly.

Cohen pulled off at the next exit, stopping at a gas station. He turned the car off, the sound of it clicking the only thing we could hear as we all sat there. Cohen turned in his seat, taking my hands.

"Fin, we do know one another. We just need to learn the details of things. But I know who you are to your core, and you know me. We spent hours getting to know the real parts of us as we chatted and became friends. The facts of my life are things anyone can learn from a simple google search, but the aspects of my personality, which Spice Girl was my favorite, and my all-time favorite movie, are the things that really define me. Those are the things you know, and not many others do."

I could hear the sincerity as he spoke, and I knew I was probably freaking out about something that didn't matter, but the mere fact that I didn't know these things made the perfectionist in me feel like a failure.

"So, you do have a sister you've never met?" I

asked. He nodded, his eyes closing as emotion seemed to take hold of his body.

"Yeah." He opened his eyes, swallowing. "I was adopted by an amazing couple, but I felt like I was still missing something. I looked into my family history when I first started hacking and found that my biological family had been killed in a car crash. I had an older sister. She was five years old when she died. I'd been left with a sitter at the time."

"Oh my God. I'm so sorry, Cohen." I moved my hands to cup his face. His scruff felt nice under my palms, and I traced my thumb over his cheek.

"It's okay. It's hard to miss a family you never knew. But it explained why I felt like a part of me was gone. I was convinced it wasn't an accident, my brain wanting to find a conspiracy, but it was. Just a drunk driver. Wrong place, wrong time, type of thing."

He shrugged his shoulders, and even though he said he was fine and over it, I felt like it was only partially the truth. Pulling him to me, I wrapped my arms around him in an embrace, wanting him to know he wasn't alone. After a while, we pulled back, and he looked lighter.

"Thanks," he whispered. Cohen cleared his throat, turning to Asa. "How'd you know I was a millionaire?"

Asa laughed, raising one shoulder. "I gotta keep my secrets, man." Cohen broke out into laughter, lifting his fist to Asa's.

"Fair enough. Alright, I'm going to get gas. It's your chance to get any snacks and go to the restroom."

Asa and I climbed out, stretching as we made our way in. After a quick pit stop, I grabbed a soda and a few sweets and headed to the counter. Cohen was already there waiting. I placed them on the counter and pulled his face down toward mine. I pecked his lips before I walked out, swishing my hips. I stopped at the door, looking over my shoulder at him.

Both Cohen and Asa were watching me. Cohen had a look of shock that turned to glee as he regained his composure. Asa seemed to be delighted, looking at me with love. Blowing a kiss, I headed out to the car, leaving them to take care of the snacks.

They joined me a few seconds later, handing out the goodies, and we got back on the road. The game never picked back up after that, but the atmosphere felt lighter as we took turns being the DJ and singing along.

It was late into the evening when we pulled up to a hotel. Cohen got out to get our room, and I sat back, realizing I was beginning to hate hotel rooms.

"You okay, Fin?" Asa asked, leaning forward again.

"Yeah, I think so. I'm glad you're here."

"Me too," he said. Asa opened his mouth to say something else, but the door opening had him closing it, and we exited, grabbing our meager belongings. We'd stopped and picked up a few things for me, so I at least had clean clothes, but they wouldn't last long if my track record was anything to go by.

Jumping up on Asa's back, I smiled, hugging him as he carried me up the stairs. Thoughts of Blackhawk began to flood me again, the hope I'd catch him on Tuesday filling me with glee. At least this time, I wouldn't be alone, which felt like all the difference.

I WAS RUNNING THROUGH A MAZE. I was being chased by a goose and it kept poking me in the back. Knocking it away, I kept running until I fell over, tripping on a log. I jumped when I landed, my body twitching, making my eyes open. That was when I realized it had been a dream and I wasn't actually being chased in a maze.

My heart started to slow at the knowledge, my breathing evening out. It took me a few seconds to realize where I was and who I was with. Two bodies pressed against me in the dim light. Unlike yesterday morning, they were both still in bed with me.

Yes, both.

I wanted to laugh at the fact that Cohen had gotten a room with only one bed, but it also didn't surprise me. He was mischievous to his core, and I knew it was his way of pushing my boundaries a little. I couldn't say I minded.

Snuggling back into the chest and arms wrapped around me, I realized, too late, that the poking hadn't been part of my dream but my reality.

A soft moan sounded out, and the body moved, rubbing itself against me. My breath caught as I felt their hand grip my stomach. Opening my eyes, I realized Asa was in front of me. Which meant… at some point in the night, I'd rolled over into Cohen's arms.

And now he was stabbing me with his very prominent morning wood.

Fingers splayed out across my tummy, pressing into me with a firm touch. They stayed there for a few seconds before they shifted slightly, moving lower, and I knew he was no longer asleep. Biting my lip, I debated if I was ready for this.

I knew Cohen. I liked Cohen. I always had, but something kept making me stall.

Was it just fear? Keeping me on this side of what I thought was okay? Or was it something more? The hard part was I wasn't sure. Years of suppressed emotions made me unable to know what I was genuinely feeling now.

I felt him move closer, his embrace feeling so safe that my body naturally relaxed into his arms. Deciding to let go and live, I didn't stop him. They both wanted me to trust them, which started with trusting myself.

When he stalled a second later, I placed my hand over his, moving it down to the hem of my sleep shorts. His tongue brushed the nape of my neck, eliciting shivers throughout me. Goosebumps spread over my arms, my nipples pebbled as they rubbed against the tee-shirt, and I bit down on my lip harder to contain a moan that wanted to slip out.

His hot breath came out in puffs as he began to creep ever so slowly beneath the elastic band. I'd never cursed myself so much for wearing shorts to bed. At the time, it seemed like the sensible thing to do. But when I wanted the boy I was too afraid to admit I liked to touch me, they felt like the world's largest chastity belt.

Cohen's pinky brushed against the cotton of my panties, no doubt feeling the wetness already present. I couldn't hide how turned on I was from the simple touch he'd given me. I was so wound up that I felt ready to combust. Holding my breath, it felt like a lifetime as he peeked his finger around the material and touched my folds.

My body responded in kind, and I bucked back into him, rubbing against his hard length. The moan I'd been trying to contain slipped out, and I re-opened my eyes to find Asa watching me. Guilt crept up my spine, and I locked my legs, my body tensing. Cohen froze, feeling me shift. My eyes grew huge, but Asa moved closer and grabbed my chin, bringing our faces closer.

"Relax, Fin." He kissed me, and I melted, my body doing as he said into the arms of Cohen, who responded in kind. But as Asa's hands weaved into my hair, kissing me like a man starved, he slowly began to move.

Asa kissed me deeply, wrapping his tongue around mine in a passionate caress. It had only been a month since I'd last kissed him this way, our earlier ones mere pecks to the panty-melting one he was giving me now. As our tongues battled, I mourned for the time we'd lost. It might have only been a month, but it felt longer. Probably because even though I'd been with him, I'd been pulling away for months.

Having shared some of the sins of my past mistakes, it had taken a wall down between us I hadn't realized was there. Kissing Asa now almost felt like the first time because I was kissing him as me and not the girl I was pretending to be.

Cohen's hand began to graze between my lower lips, pulling some of the wetness with him as he moved up and down. The teasing was driving me wild, and I tried to move closer to make him touch me more. His other hand gripped my hip, holding me still.

"Patience, sweetheart."

I groaned, making Asa chuckle as he pulled away and lifted my shirt. His tongue began to peek out, licking my stiff peaks, teasing me along with Cohen.

"If one of you doesn't fully touch me, I'm boycotting you both."

"Oh, I think someone doesn't like us teaming up," Cohen teased, biting my earlobe.

"This wasn't the type of team-up I had in mind," I gritted out.

Cohen's grip on my hip tightened, and he pulled me back into his cock, the hard length rubbing against my ass. Gasping, I clamped down the urge to rock more, hoping he'd reward me if I stayed the course. His finger dipped between my pussy lips, flicking over my clit, and I bit my lip, praying he'd finally push further.

Asa moved closer, taking my breast into his mouth; my back arched, making Cohen's finger slip further into my core. When he finally moved it in and out, it was the sweetest pressure, making me want to weep in relief. His thumb found my clit, and his finger began to plunge in me deeply as Asa sucked my nipple. I rocked into them both, wanting more but knowing we weren't there yet. This was a huge first step, and I needed to take it for what it was and not push myself too much too soon, even if my body was screaming for more.

It didn't take long once Cohen began to spear me, and I found myself grasping Asa's head to my chest as I began to spasm, a cry of pleasure leaving my mouth.

"Fuck, sweetheart, you make the sweetest sounds. I can't wait to hear more," Cohen whispered, licking up my neck again. I shivered, no longer trying to hide how my body responded to him. He pulled his finger out slowly, the sensation making my eyes roll back, and for some reason, I wasn't surprised when he sucked down my juices like a desperate man. It was primal and seductive, making me wish they were still in me so I could ride them again.

"Good morning," Asa whispered, pulling me closer, not caring at all about Cohen. It eased the last shred of hesitancy I had out of me that he was being honest about his feelings. I guess I owed it to myself to be real then. If Asa was willing to let me be open with my heart, then I needed to brave and open it and stop hiding behind him.

"I'm not sure which is better to wake up to," I said, a smile on my face. "An orgasm, or coffee and donuts."

The boys snickered, knowing I was full of shit,

but it eased the tension as we got out of bed and dressed. It was time to find Blackhawk.

SCREAMS OF JOY and the rush of rides as they went around, hit us as we walked into the Raven Time theme park. It took a minute to orient myself to the surroundings, the environment so different from what I was used to.

"It's very loud," Cohen said, his nose scrunching up as he looked around. "And bright."

Asa had a massive smile on his face as he took it all in. "That's because you tend to be more of a vampire hermit and only come out at night. Come on, we have a bit of time before we need to meet him. Let's scope out the area and maybe go on a few rides. Might as well have some fun while we're here."

He bounded off, full of energy, and it was at times like this that I wondered how he dated me. While he had the energy of Sawyer, my best friend, Asa, also had a lightness about him that was utterly him.

"Is it me, or is it weird how happy he is all the time?"

Snorting, I hit him in the stomach. "You're the weird one. Asa is a good one. Don't knock it."

Cohen rolled his eyes but smiled, tugging me

along as we followed Asa. He stopped and looked at each sign, reading everything and taking it all in. It was cute.

"Oh, this!" he said, pointing to a pretty empty line. I looked at the sign, trying to read what it was.

"Rock-n-Roll Riders?" I shrugged, the name doing nothing to tell me what the ride was about. Cohen sighed but agreed and followed us into the line. We didn't have to wait long as we made it to the front and stood behind the metal bars until the ride appeared. Everyone who got off seemed happy and full of smiles, so I took that as a good sign.

Asa pulled my hand, going for the front of the ride when we were allowed to enter. Cohen dragged his feet behind us, and I didn't know if it was because he wasn't used to being up this early or something else. It was a three-person cart, so we slid in, with me in the middle. Asa pulled the bar down, an excited look on his face as he peered over at me. When he looked at Cohen, though, he frowned, and I turned to see what it was about.

"You okay, man?" he asked. "You don't look so good."

"Hmm, mm," he replied, his eyes shut tight. Grasping his hand, I threaded our fingers together and pulled his head to look at me.

"You okay?"

"So, confession time. I've never been on a roller coaster, and I'm kind of afraid of heights."

Sympathy for him filled me, and I squeezed his hand. "You can get off," I started, right as the attendant came and tugged our bar, deeming it was good.

"You're good," he said, tapping the cart, and in the next second, we were off. I turned back to the front, holding Asa's hand as the ride began to move. It was slow at first as it crept up, and I peeked over at Cohen, his eyes still closed tight.

I could feel us climbing, and I knew a big dip was coming, so I decided to be brave. Taking a breath, I quickly kissed Asa on the cheek and let go of his hand. He smiled, nodding, having figured out what I was going to do.

I cupped Cohen's face as we came to the top, his eyes remaining closed. "Cohen, look."

He shook his head, so I decided to go all in. As we began to crest over the edge, I pulled his lips to mine. I kept my eyes open, wanting to see if he would look. Pressing my lips into his, he stayed frozen for a few seconds, and I felt us beginning to plummet down. Shouts of glee rang out around us, my stomach climbing to my throat as we dropped, but I kept pressing, holding him to me.

After a few seconds, he opened his eyes, and I felt as if I had seen Cohen Campbell for the first time.

There were no barriers, no banter to hide behind, just raw vulnerability.

He stared back, and something in him switched, and I caught a fire burning. His hands swept up into my hair, pulling me closer to him as the roller coaster turned and wheeled around bends. Asa's hand gripped my leg, but outside of that touch, I felt like I was floating as Cohen kissed me back.

It was aggressive and rough; his tongue sought dominance as he took over the kiss, not asking for permission but taking the kiss he wanted. When we started to slow, he drew back, panting a little as we stared.

"I think roller coasters just became my favorite thing," he said, his eyes bright and his smile wide as he peered back at me.

"Me too."

The three of us climbed off, rode a few other rides, played a couple of games, and grabbed food as we walked around. When the sun began to shift lower, I knew the time for fun and games was over.

"I guess we should head to the funhouse," I said, sighing.

"The fact he picked a funhouse is creepy within itself," Asa said, swinging my hand. I'd been holding hands with both of them all day, not caring as people would stop and look. It felt nice to not let other people dictate how I should act.

"That wasn't in the book, was it?" Cohen asked.

"No. I don't recall it being there. They went to the Ferris wheel and ate cotton candy." I shrugged.

The sign for the funhouse grew bigger the closer we got, a new pit forming in my stomach. It felt wrong somehow. Everything Blackhawk and I had up until this point had felt more, but maybe that was my misguided attempt to not feel like I'd been duped like the world's biggest loser.

"You ready?" Asa asked, looking at me.

"I dunno. It feels strange. What if we didn't get the clue right?"

"Then we go back and reassess. You're not in this alone."

Taking a big breath in, I nodded, feeling confident with their presence that this time it wouldn't be too late.

"One at a time," the attendant said, stopping Asa from following me.

"We'll be right behind you," he said, and I swallowed.

Stepping into the funhouse, I took hold of the railing as it began to tilt, throwing my balance off-center. Mirrors and lights around me began to move, making my depth perception off, and I struggled to walk in a straight line.

I couldn't turn to see how the guys were doing, so I focused on taking one step at a time, looking only at the ground. When I got to a hallway, I sighed in relief, the topsy-turvy feeling dissipating. Turning, I was surprised when I found myself alone and when I took a step, I smacked into a mirror.

"Ow! How?"

What I thought had been the way I'd come was now closed off, a mirror in its place. I spun around, all the mirrors showing different reflections of me in a kaleidoscope of Fin's.

Frantically, I began to stumble as I searched for a way out, a way back to the guys. My breathing became ragged as anxiety began to overtake me, and flashbacks of past times began to collide with reality, making me confused about what was real and what wasn't.

I caught a flash of black out of the corner of my eye, and I turned, searching for it. Tears streamed down my face as I tried to find someone. I was so dizzy, I could barely see.

"Please, I don't want to be here."

A body pressed up against my back, a hand covering my mouth, and I began to thrash. I felt something begin to prick my neck, a cold feeling settling in me that I was being drugged again. But when I blinked, it was gone, and the body left me.

Sucking in a breath, I took the chance and darted forward, finally seeing my way out.

But I'd been wrong. Again.

Smacking my face into the mirror, I saw two figures fighting, but I didn't know if that was my imagination, or reality once again. Before I could investigate, the pain encompassed me, my eyes sliding closed as everything went dark.

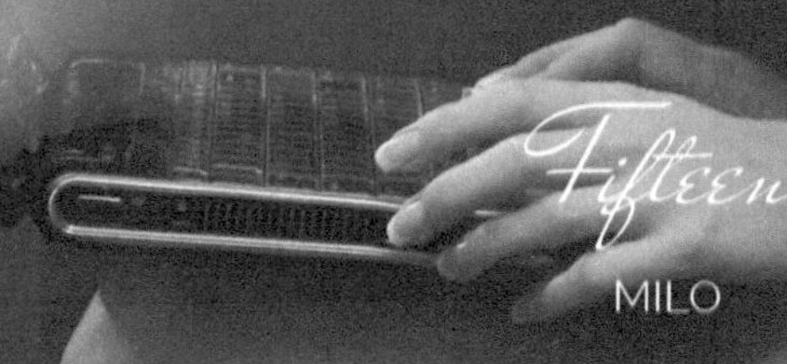

MY LIFE HAD NEVER BEEN easy, so debating the dilemma I was currently faced with should've been effortless. But I was finding Finley Reyes to be anything but easy.

From the moment I met her, I felt a spark ignite in me that hadn't been lit in years. Being a Bellamy, expectations were placed on my shoulders from birth. As I grew, I bucked against them as much as possible, trying to find my own path. Over time, having to fight for the simplest thing wore me down. I hadn't realized how tired and stagnant I'd become until I was helping two girls who'd been taken against their will and being forced to be part of a human auction.

It was at that moment I knew I couldn't continue down the path I was on, attempting to play both sides—living the life I wanted by becoming a doctor and fulfilling family commitments when called upon. I'd ignored the more sinister side of things, pretending they didn't exist, but I couldn't ignore it any longer in that dark underground facility.

The Bellamys were criminals, and if I turned my head, I was just as bad.

Helping Finley was the first step in taking a stand against them and separating myself from my family. Over the past year, I'd become financially independent, setting myself apart from the Bellamys. After the Council had been taken down, it was necessary as everything connected to them was seized by the authorities, leaving the once flourishing Bellamy line barren.

And today, I would make the last stand against them, finalizing my separation from a family of crooks and murderers.

"Dr. Milo Bellamy," the chancellor announced, and I smiled, walking up the stage to shake his hand. He handed me my diploma, and I walked over a few feet, moving my tassel to the other side. Posing for the photographer, I smiled into the camera, the weight of my achievements sitting proudly on my shoulders.

I'd done it. This had been all me.

Walking back down the steps, I shook hands with

a few of my professors before making it back to my seat. Some of my classmates congratulated me in passing, patting me on the back. I wasn't that close with most of them, having kept to myself, too afraid of being used for my family. It was a lonely life, always being mistrustful of others.

It was why Finley had been such a breath of fresh air. But as that one '90s song went, as soon as I thought I'd met the girl of my dreams, I was introduced to her perfect boyfriend. It was ironic that the first girl I liked was someone I had to rescue from my family.

Since then, I'd been wrestling with my feelings, while trying to be the friend she needed. It was nice, actually, because I got to be in her life without much commitment.

But for the first time, I wanted more. I wanted her to expect things from me. I wanted to be counted on. This past month, I wondered if I'd finally have a chance.

She'd reached out to *me*, needing *my* help.

Finley Reyes made it easy to ride in on the white horse and rescue her.

"Congratulations, graduates!" the chancellor cheered, and everyone rose to their feet, tossing their caps into the air. I followed suit, but I couldn't deny it felt lonely. I'd worked so hard to be seen as a nobody, so I wouldn't be taken advantage of, that now, when I'd succeeded, I realized how sucky it actually felt to be alone.

Perhaps it was time to step up my game. I didn't know what was going on with Fin, but I couldn't deny my feelings for her had grown. This could be my one chance to show her I could be depended on as more than her friend.

Decision made and my dilemma over, I headed to my car, not even bothering with pleasantries as I made my way there. It would be unlikely that I'd see any of my classmates again, especially since my residency was on the West Coast. There wasn't anything left for me in Boston.

Tossing the black gown and diploma case into the passenger seat of my car, I revved the engine as I pulled out my phone and clicked on the icon for Fin. She didn't know I'd done this, but it felt like the safest bet to keep tabs on her with no one else knowing where she was currently. It was merely for her safety.

Yeah, I didn't buy it either.

When her location showed her only a few hours away at an amusement park, I became even more curious about what she was up to. It would take too long to drive, even in my sports car, so I made a left at the end of the road and headed toward the airport.

As much as I hated my family at times, I couldn't deny that I'd learned to use my resources wisely. It was time to use some of my money to charter a jet. For some reason, I had a weird sensation that it was crucial I made it to her location today.

THE SUN WAS STARTING to set as I stepped into Raven Time. Even though the park closed soon, it was still full of families and teenagers as they hurriedly rushed from one side to the next, desperate to get in one more go before the rides shut down. The smell of cotton candy, funnel cakes, and fried chicken filled the space as I walked through the park, looking for the woman who'd stolen my heart.

In a naive way, I'd thought I'd be able to feel her, my body being automatically drawn to hers. But I didn't see her anywhere, so I pulled out my phone in desperation, hoping I could pinpoint a more precise location.

"That can't be right," I muttered, looking around since the damn thing said I was right where she was. The only thing here was a funhouse and a hot dog stand, and Finley wasn't anywhere. Shouting at the front of the line drew my attention, and I recognized the two guys. They were fighting with the attendant to let them through, saying they were with the girl who'd gone in already.

"Sorry, it's full. You have to wait until that party is out." The kid didn't care that two guys twice his size were demanding to be let in. I'd respect the kid if it wasn't at Fin's expense.

Knowing that nothing good could be occurring if Asa and Cohen were blocked off from the front, I made a split-second decision to circumvent the line and go around to the back. It might be selfish not to let them know I was here or that I was finding a different route, but I couldn't deny I wanted to be the one to rush in.

Fuck, I really needed to find another way to show her I cared. I'd think about it later when I knew she wasn't in danger.

The loud generator blocked all sound from the front as I looked around the building. Trash littered the ground as I made my way around it. A little way down, I discovered a side door standing ajar, so I peeked in. Finding no one around, I slipped in and took a few seconds to orient myself to the darkness.

Music could be heard from the front, so I followed it, realizing I was behind the attractions. Every so often, there would be a door, so I'd open it and look in to see if it was where Fin was. I found myself in the mirrors at the third door, and I instantly cringed as a hundred different versions of me glared back.

It made it more difficult to look around with all the distortions. Squinting, I saw a shape lying on the ground, but it was far away. Closing the door I'd opened, I quickly went to the next to find two guys fighting. Shutting it, I kept going, praying that one of them would open closer to the prone figure.

On the fifth one, I struck gold and was able to see the person lying on the ground better. Making my way around a few mirrors, I kneeled down, brushing the hair back. A spike of fear rushed through me when I realized it was Fin. The two figures I'd seen earlier moved closer, and I had an odd feeling they were fighting over the girl lying on the ground.

Picking her up, I made my way back to the door, thankful I'd remembered which turns I'd made since it looked the same in the mirror maze. When the door shut, the music was dulled, giving me a slight reprieve to look down at the girl in my arms. She made a small moan, but it was enough to let me know she was still alive. Going back the way I'd come, I counted the doors as I passed until I went to the one on the opposite side that led outside.

When I exited the house of horrors, I looked around, searching for a place to lay her down. A nearby picnic table by the hot dog stand caught my eye, and I walked over, laying her on top of it. The yelling at the front of the line was still going on, and I realized Asa and Cohen were still trying to get inside. Placing my fingers in my mouth, I let out a big whistle, drawing their attention.

I motioned for them to come over, pointing at the table. It took them a few seconds to recognize me, but once they saw Fin's prone body, they quickly gave up their quest to argue with the teenage attendant and jumped over the railing to get out of line.

While they made their way to me, I checked Fin over, taking her pulse and inspecting her body for any signs of injury. There didn't seem to be any visible signs of trauma outside a knot on her forehead.

"Milo?" Asa asked, slightly out of breath as he reached me. "How?" he started, but then shook his head. "Actually, explain later. Is she okay?"

"I think so. She was unconscious when I found her. It looks like she might've hit her head. Her pulse is a little fast, and she's pale, but that could be from passing out." I lifted her eyelids, finding her pupils responded to the light, and a sigh of relief fell from my lips. "I think she's okay, for the most part."

I looked up, meeting the two guys who were watching me. They didn't look pissed, so I relaxed, no longer worried I'd get a black eye.

"I can tell you both have questions, but the fact that you were both still out there and that when I found her, two other guys were fighting, I'd suggest we go somewhere else for the conversation."

Whatever they'd been about to say died off, and they both went into hyperdrive, focused on Fin. I appreciated that they took what I was saying seriously and didn't hesitate to respond. Maybe this wouldn't be as horrible as I imagined.

Though I hadn't expected two other guys to be present when I shared my heart, it seemed like I'd have to get used to it or move on. I was beginning to realize I couldn't move on.

Asa bent down and picked up Fin into his arms. I wanted to pout for losing the opportunity to do so, but this wasn't the time. I followed them out of the park, and I peeked back, something drawing my attention as we turned the corner. I couldn't be sure, but it looked like one of the figures from the tussle was standing in the shadows, watching us.

Stopping, I looked closer, but nothing but darkness greeted me, the last light of the sun having disappeared.

"Milo?" Cohen shouted, and I turned back, jogging to catch up to where they'd stopped.

"Nothing, I thought I saw something," I said in response to their looks. The three of us made our way out of the park with nothing more to say, ignoring looks as Asa carried Finley.

I'd come here thinking I'd share my heart with a girl, praying I wouldn't be rejected. And instead, I was possibly finding myself part of something bigger. All I knew was if Fin was involved, I was all in. It was time I stopped being just her rescuer and showed her I was here to stay.

Sixteen

FINLEY

PAIN THROBBED IN MY TEMPLE, and I wanted to move so I could make it stop, but my arms were banded to my sides by a strong force. Voices shouted nearby, and I tried to recall the last thing that had happened, but nothing outside of the pain filtered through.

A whimper left my lips, acting as a warning sign to the noise as it abruptly stopped. The tightness holding me shifted, a warm sensation spreading over my forehead.

"Fin, sweetheart, you awake?" a voice asked, sounding miles away. I felt like a kid with a string and a can, waiting for the garbled message to reach me, but it didn't make sense when it did.

Painfully, I used all my strength to lift one eye open, only to be blinded by a light shining into it.

Wincing, I drew back, smacking into the hard object that held me. Another whimper left me as I tried to figure out what was happening. Memories coursed through my head of my kidnapping as fear rose up in me, coating my skin in a cold sweat.

"No!" I shouted, but the sound only came out as a muffled scream.

Soothing sounds and soft touches bracketed my face as the pressure from behind let up. The now gentle compression felt nice, calming my racing heart and breathing. As I began to feel more like myself, I decided to try opening my eyes again. Slowly, I lifted my eyelid, thankful that I wasn't blinded by light this time. A face swam into focus, the edges of a smile playing on their lips.

"Asa," I sighed, my body relaxing. His comforting smell of rain and cotton filled my nostrils as I breathed him in. My hands reached out, clasping onto him, not wanting to be left alone.

"You're okay, Fin. You're safe. We got you," a voice behind me said, reminding me that there had been someone there. I peeked over my shoulder to find Cohen smiling at me.

"What happened?"

"What do you remember?" a third voice asked. Asa leaned to the left, and the owner of the little flashlight came into view.

"Milo! You're here?"

I tried to sit up, but Cohen's arms had reclaimed their position around me, keeping me pressed to his chest. It felt awkward to be held by him in front of Milo, and I didn't know why. I reasoned that I didn't want Milo to feel uncomfortable, but even that sounded off to my own mind.

"He's the one that found you, sweetheart," Cohen cooed, brushing my hair behind my ear as he whispered into it. "He saved you."

"That sounds about right," I mumbled. Dropping my eyes, I looked at the bedspread, trying to place where we were. It looked like the one from our hotel room. That knowledge seemed to help me relax completely, and my brain began to think again.

I was safe. I was safe. I was safe.

Now that I knew I wasn't being kidnapped again, the flashes of memory began to trickle through. The funhouse and the masked man that'd grabbed me.

"Where did you find me?" I asked, needing to know more information.

"You were unconscious in the middle of a funhouse," Milo answered, sitting on the bed. I watched as his hand flexed, almost like he wanted to reach out and take mine. Deciding he'd earned a little hand-holding, I reached out and took his before remembering he wasn't part of the dating deal.

I sucked in a breath, watching out of the corner of my eye to see what the others would do. When no one tensed, got angry, or punched Milo, I decided to take it as a win for now and would deal with it more later. Milo appeared to be on the same page as his grip tightened in mine.

"Okay, well, I guess that's good that I didn't get taken far. So, were you the one who attacked Blackhawk?"

"Blackhawk?" he asked before shaking his head. "I don't know who that is, but I didn't attack anyone. Two guys were fighting when I found you. I didn't stop to ask them their names."

Something about the way he said that had a giggle leaving my lips, and his shoulders relaxed, a smile spreading across his handsome face. I took him in, noticing him in more detail. He was dressed in a button-down shirt, bow tie, and dress pants. He looked really handsome, not helping with my 'wanting more than I should' problem.

"You look really nice," I blurted, my cheeks heating. Cheese cracker! I was turning into Sawyer.

"Oh, thanks." He glanced down like he'd just realized what he was wearing. "I didn't really have time to change before heading here."

"How did you know to come?" I asked, finally realizing how odd it was he was here. "And what were you doing beforehand?" I scrunched my nose, groaning when it hurt, remembering the throbbing from earlier. My hand reached up to touch the spot, but Asa grabbed it, locking it in his. I was now being touched by three guys, and my vagina started to get ideas.

"I, uh…" He blushed even more, and I wondered if he could read my thoughts or if I'd voiced it all out loud, and my own face began to redden in response.

"It's kind of an embarrassing story. Can we maybe talk about what happened to you first? I want to make sure you're okay."

"After you went into the funhouse, the attendant wouldn't let us through," Asa began, pulling us back to the topic. "He kept saying that the party was full and we had to wait. What happened once you were inside?"

I blinked, trying to recall the events. They all slammed into me, my eyes closing at the onslaught.

"It was weird. Everything was trippy, and it took me a while to get my equilibrium. The mirrors played tricks, and I thought it was one of you, but then a guy was behind me. I don't remember much other than him placing a hand over my mouth. There was a little pinch in my neck, but then it was gone. I thought one of you had come in, so I took the chance to run. What I assumed was the way out wasn't, and I smacked into the mirror at full speed. I'm guessing that's where I got this." I tilted my head since I didn't have the use of my hands. "Your turn."

The guys all looked at each other, apparently not knowing who I was speaking to. A smile spread across my face, and despite the situation, it felt nice to be surrounded by them all. But as soon as the thought entered my head, I pushed it away. I couldn't get too comfortable thinking I could keep all three.

The realization had me sobering, and I dropped a hand to tap Cohen's arm. He made a grumble, the possessiveness doing something to my insides.

"Can I sit up, please?"

"Fine," he replied, the sound more like a growl than a real answer. He let go of me, and everyone repositioned themselves on the bed as I sat up. I briefly glanced around, trying to buy time as I took in the details of our room.

Putting my hands in my lap, I peered back at Cohen and Asa. "Did you get a good look at Blackhawk? Where is he? Did he get away?"

They both seemed to drop their eyes as Asa shook his head. "We didn't get him."

"But, I thought..." Cohen sighed, his whole body collapsing like a deflated balloon.

"We never made it inside. We don't know who the other person was."

The knowledge that an unknown person had saved me felt odd. Was it coincidental? Had they been trailing Blackhawk too? Or was it just a good Samaritan?

"Oh," I finally said, playing with the cover. "Hmm, so." Looking up at the guys, I noticed their faces reflected mine. "Yeah, I got nothing. Okay, so first Milo tells us where he was and how he found me, and then Cohen and I will see if we can find anything out from any cameras."

"Already ahead of you there. They were turned off during that time frame. Which makes me think it was Blackhawk, at least. He'd know how to do that."

My shoulders slumped, and I drew in a deep breath. "Right, fine, we'll worry about that later. Milo?"

He smiled, shaking his head as his cheeks heated again. "You're not going to let it go, are you?"

"Nope. Sorry, but it's easier to focus on that than almost being kidnapped again." That seemed to sober the guys and Milo nodded, exhaling.

"First, I, um, kind of graduated today." He brushed his fingers through his hair in a nervous gesture, and I felt jealous of them.

"Wow, congratulations, man!" Asa cheered, slapping him on the back. And once again, my perfect boyfriend reminded me what the proper response was in this situation, and it wasn't fixating on fingers.

"Congrats, Milo. Or, I guess, Dr. Milo. I'm so happy for you." He smiled at me, some relief on his face.

"Yeah, well, it feels good to do something outside of my family. But when I looked around the crowd, I realized how well I'd done at pushing everyone away so they couldn't take advantage of me. I was there, alone, with no one to take a picture with. And it just felt like it didn't even matter. If no one witnesses your success, is it a success?"

"Of course it is. Don't let them take this from you too. We should celebrate."

"You're right, and that's how I ended up here. I knew who I wanted to celebrate with." He ducked his head, his cheeks returning to that adorable shade of red.

"How did you know where I was, though?"

I conveniently ignored the other part that, out of all the people in the world, I was the one he wanted to celebrate his accomplishment with.

"Does it matter?" Asa asked. He looked at me, a serious look in his eyes. "He saved you. Without him," he shuddered, stopping his words as thoughts flitted across his eyelids, "you might not be sitting here with us now. So, you two can talk about it later, but I'm glad he showed up when he did. And personally, I think that calls for some pizza and beer. How does that sound for a mini-celebration tonight?" he asked, turning to Milo.

It was killing me not knowing the answer, but I recognized what Asa was saying and doing. He was including Milo in our little circle, and I needed to honor what that meant. I could talk with Milo later, but maybe Asa was right about not needing to know as well.

Looking up, I found that Milo had been watching me. I gave him a soft smile, letting him know I wasn't angry. It seemed to be what he needed as he turned to Asa, and they started to talk about pizza toppings. Cohen took the opportunity to pull me back to his chest.

Tilting my head, I looked at the man I was getting to know on a whole new level. "I never took you as a cuddle person."

"Oh? Was it the stellar wit that keeps people at arm's length or the all-black attire that made you take that leap?" he asked, smirking at me.

Snuggling into his arms, I found him to be rather comfortable. "Hm, more of the 'I'm too cool for school' attitude."

Cohen laughed, his breath making the top of my

hair move. "Yeah, well, it's probably a lot of things. I kept people at arm's length on purpose. But deep down, I'm a big softie who's a physical person. I knew if I ever let myself get too close then, I wouldn't be able to let you go, and for the longest time, I didn't think you were an option."

"I'm glad you didn't run away," I whispered, my eyes drawing heavy again as I listened to his heartbeat.

"Everywhere I ran, it always led me back to you. I'm not going anywhere, sweetheart. I will cuddle your ass until you're old and gray."

"That's kind of sweet in a morbid way." I yawned, shifting a little.

"Ssh, close your eyes. I'll wake you when the food is here."

He pressed his lips to my forehead, and I took his advice, letting myself fall back under. At least this time, I was safe and surrounded by three guys who would do whatever it took to protect me. Like Milo, I was learning that some things were better with people. And this was definitely one of them.

THE SMELL of melted cheese and pepperoni tickled my nose, waking me. Cohen's warm body still pressed into me, and I stayed still for a moment, enjoying the comfort of his embrace.

"Where should we eat it?" one of the guys asked quietly. "The table is only big enough for the box."

"True, it looks like the bed or floor then."

I heard them gathering things, and I debated if I should get up and help. Usually, that was my role, the one who made sure everything was taken care of and ready to go. But I couldn't deny that it felt nice to let someone else take charge for once.

"I know you're awake, sweetheart."

Turning my head into his chest, I felt his laugh rumble through me. "You're comfy." I yawned, nuzzling down in him.

"Good to know. Pizza's here." I could practically hear the smirk in his voice.

"Mm," I mumbled, shaking my head.

When my stomach growled, I sighed, moving to sit up, no longer able to ignore the hunger. I found all three guys focused on me when I opened my eyes. Blinking, I realized that sleeping as many times as I did in my contacts wasn't cutting it anymore, and they were dry as a bone.

"Um, give me a minute."

I slid off the bed and padded over to the bathroom. Shutting the door behind me, I leaned against it for a second. There were so many emotions racing through me that I didn't know where to start.

"Right, first deal with the most pressing matters," I said aloud, the habit not completely broken yet.

Taking a second to relieve myself, I quickly took out my contacts and tossed them into the trash. Placing my glasses on my face, I looked at myself in the mirror, taking in my features. My skin was pale, the bump standing out on my forehead. Brushing my hair over, I covered it for the most part. My nose stud shined in the light as I turned back and forth. Despite my paleness, my eyes seemed bright and alert, and I could only attribute that to the three men in the other room.

Pushing my shoulders back, I took a deep breath

and left the relative safety of the bathroom. Their chatter stopped when I emerged, both making me happy and suspicious. I was glad they weren't at odds, but what did three guys who were practically strangers have to talk about besides me?

Which led me to believe they were talking about me.

"Um, it smells good. Shall we?" I asked, sitting back in my spot on the bed. Asa nodded, lifting the lid. He frowned, leaning closer.

"Did they put on the wrong toppings?" Cohen asked.

Milo leaned with him, his eyes widened before glancing up at me. I was beyond curious at this point, so I peered around the raised lid, pulling it back.

"Did we get pizza boobs? Sawyer got cake boobs once."

Asa let it fall, making me appreciate the fact he wasn't trying to hide this. An envelope with my name was taped to the inside of the box. So, not boobs.

"Wow, that's not creepy," I said.

"I don't even want to know what cake boobs are," Asa said grimacing.

Laughing at his discomfort, I ripped off the envelope and held it in my hand. I knew it had to be from *him*. The weight of that knowledge felt heavy in my hands, and I debated if I wanted to open this or not. I hadn't processed what happened at the funhouse yet, but clearly, if he was willing to drug me and take me, we weren't playing on the same levels anymore.

Was it even worth continuing this fight? Did I want to risk my life to get my revenge? Maybe I needed to accept I was out of my league and move on.

"Are you going to open it?" Cohen asked, squeezing my leg close to him.

I looked up, shrugging. "I don't know. I think I should just stop. It doesn't feel as worth it anymore. The stakes are too high." I tapped the letter on my knee, the corner poking into my skin. The slight pressure helped ground me so I didn't spiral into a million places.

"Did you see who delivered the pizza?" Cohen asked, not responding to me.

"It was just left at the front desk," Asa said, frowning as he began to think. I watched as he ran his hand through his blond locks, his green eyes staring off into the distance.

Cohen jumped off the bed, grabbing his computer and bringing it back over. He started to type in some things as I stared back at the envelope. Milo nudged my foot, making me look up. The pizza box in between us had been left abandoned. I wasn't sure if it was even safe to eat it at this point. It was sad to waste pizza.

"You want me to read it with you?" he asked. I peered into his dark brown eyes behind his silver frames, wondering if when two people who wore glasses kissed, they scratched one another.

He grasped my foot this time, shaking it again. "Fin?"

"Huh?" Oh, right, he'd asked me a question, and I'd gotten distracted by thoughts of kissing. "Yeah, I guess."

I shrugged, not really knowing how to feel at this point. He moved over, our thighs touching, and I liked how that felt. I couldn't deny that no matter what I got out of the end of this, I at least had faced my feelings.

His hand landed on my thigh, and he squeezed it, letting me know he was here. Taking a deep breath, I flipped it over and pushed my thumb under the flap, tearing it.

Once it was open, I stared at the folded paper, not yet quite ready to pull it out. Sucking in a breath, I let it out slowly, feeling more calm. Carefully, I slid out the paper, letting it fall to my lap. With each step, I seemed to need to stop and take a breath of courage, before I could move on to the next.

I unfolded the paper with trembling fingers,

surprised when it was a letter. For some reason, I hadn't expected a letter, but more of a note with letters cut out of a magazine like a serial killer's ransom note.

Glancing over at Milo, I found his eyes watching me. He was confident and reassuring, giving me the courage to look down and read what Blackhawk had to say.

Oblivion,

I'm sorry for going to this extreme to get this to you. I promise, I only paid the guy to attach this letter. I didn't do anything to the pizza. If I know you like I think I do, that will be your first question.

I was afraid you wouldn't get online after what happened today if I didn't Send you something real.

First, congrats on figuring out the cluE. Your cleverness is one of the things I admire about you the most. I forgot how much fun we had with our puzzles and games, and *Forgotten Time* seemed like the best way to gain what we'd lost.

But something seems to have gone amiss.

You were almost hurt today, and that's never been part of the game.

I'm glad one of your suitors Could get you out

in time. Whoever is working against me is smaRt. Too smart. I have an idea, but I need to finalize it before saying anything.

Until thEn, I don't think it's wise to continue our game. I hope you understand, but your safeTy is more important than just having fun. It would've been great to meet you in person today. You looked Stunning. You've grown up to be a beautiful woman, just like I thought you would.

I'll be in touch.

See you soon,

Blackhawk

I dropped the letter onto my lap, my mind whirling with questions. Why did it sound like he wasn't the one who'd attacked me? In fact, he acted like we were just having fun? That he hadn't betrayed me all those years ago.

"It doesn't make sense."

Milo watched me, then picked up the letter, rereading it. Asa walked back into the room, a new pizza in his hand. I hadn't realized he'd left or that it had taken me that long to build up the courage to read the letter.

He took the cold pizza off the bed, closing the lid. He observed me, looking for something. I gave him a lopsided smile, hoping it would help soothe whatever had made the crease between his eyes develop.

"Thank you for getting a new pizza. He said he hadn't touched it, but..." I shrugged.

"No problem. You okay? That feels like the wrong thing to ask, but I'm not sure what else to say."

"I'm not even sure what I am. It's kind of been a day."

Asa moved closer to the bed, sitting in front of me. He pulled my legs across his lap, and I was officially cocooned by the three of them. Cohen was still busy typing on his computer. When I peeked over, he was typing code so fast I couldn't follow it. Milo folded the letter and handed it to Asa.

"What do you think?" I asked, looking up at him.

"I don't know the whole story, but it seems like he wasn't the one who was trying to take you, but the other guy, fighting him off. I think..." he shook his head, clearing something.

"What?" I asked, realizing he'd stopped himself from saying something.

"It's nothing."

"It's something," Asa said, not letting it go either.

"It's just," he sighed, looking down at me. "When we were leaving, I looked back, and it looked like one of the guys was watching. It seemed like they were making sure we got out okay. I got the sense it was more out of concern instead of wanting to follow us."

"Fuck," Cohen grumbled, slamming his laptop closed. He rubbed his head, pulling at the wavy ends. "This guy is good. He's top-level. He covers all of his bases, leaving no trail behind. If he doesn't want you to find him, you won't. I'm sorry, sweetheart."

Cohen dropped his hands, turning to look over at me. Regret sat heavy in his eyes. Taking his hand, I linked our fingers together.

"Thank you for trying."

"So, where does that leave us?" Asa asked just as my stomach growled in demand. The guys laughed, and he got up, grabbing the pizza and napkins. He lifted the lid and pulled me a piece, placing it on a plate before handing it to me.

"Thank you," I said, smiling at him. Asa taking care of me was nice.

The guys dug into their food, making the room quiet as we all fell into our own thoughts as we ate. After finishing two slices, I set my plate aside, picking up the letter again.

Staring at it, I noticed something. "It's a password," I mumbled as the letter fell together. Every so often one would be capitalized randomly.

Cohen took the letter from me, reading it over, a

smile spreading across his face as he seemed to pick up the same thing I had.

"You're right. Maybe it connects to something," he said, opening his computer. Before we could see where that led us to, a knock at the door had us all startling. Asa looked around at us, the three of us shrugging almost simultaneously, making us laugh.

Asa moved my legs from his lap and got up. I glanced over at Milo, and he had the same look I did—curiosity. Together, we crawled off the bed laughing, making it to the door just as Asa shut it. He turned, smirking when he saw we'd come to his rescue.

He lifted a black envelope, a gold script written on the outside. Moving closer, I realized it was my name.

"Another one?" I asked, reaching out for the card.

"The front desk said it was dropped off this morning with strict instructions to be delivered to our door at 8pm."

A weird feeling began to bubble up in my belly when I looked between the two. Just how out of my depth was I? I thought I could right the wrongs from my adolescence, but instead, I seemed to have stumbled into something bigger than I was capable of handling.

The three of us walked back toward the bed,

catching Cohen's attention when I stopped at the foot of it with the card. I waved it awkwardly at him.

He gulped, his eyes going wide. "Um, where did you get that?"

"It was dropped off at the front desk to be delivered this evening," Asa replied. I glanced up at him, finding he was looking at Cohen oddly. Looking back, I noticed he was more sweaty than usual. I'd assumed it was about me, but maybe Asa was picking up on something I'd failed to see.

"Do you know what this is?" I asked, not taking my eyes off him. He nodded slowly, swallowing.

Tired of all the letters I'd received today, I flipped it over, pulling up the flap. The thick cardstock ripped satisfyingly. I pulled out the black card, blinking after, sure I'd misread it.

"You're part of the Order?" I asked, putting the pieces together.

Cohen's shoulders fell, and he nodded. "I am. That company I said that saved me? The one that offered me the job when I'd been caught?"

"Yeah," I said, my throat going dry.

"It was them."

"So, you've been working for the Order the whole time?"

"Yes, but not how you're thinking. You were never part of the job, Fin. I promise. It just happened to overlap at times. The Order is secretive. You can't talk about it. So even though I've been part of it, it's not like I have an office to go back to. I work for them by working other places."

"Does Samson know?" Asa asked, his arms crossed, his eyes narrow as he stared down Cohen.

"No." He shook his head. "No one knew. I don't know anyone outside of my training class who's in the Order. Just the people I've met while there, and that's limited. Everyone uses a code name online, so I don't know who people are. It's a safety measure. I've never even met my handler face to face."

"Why didn't you say anything?"

"I can't. If you think your phone or other smart devices are listening to you, the Order is bigger than that. They're in everything, bringing balance to the corruption where they can. They would've had me taken away the next day if I had told you. You never would've seen me again."

A sadness I hadn't expected filled me at never having seen Cohen again and despite my hatred of secrets, I was glad he hadn't told me if that was the consequence.

"So, why are you telling us now?" Milo asked Cohen, and I realized he hadn't read the card.

I lifted the card, handing it to him. "Because I've been invited to join their ranks."

Finely Reyes, you're cordially invited to join
Imperium in Imperio.
We'll trust your judgment on who you share it with.
Be selective. This is your first test. You have forty-
eight hours to respond.
The Order

FINLEY

THE WIND WHIPPED AROUND ME, tossing my hair in every direction. I reached down to my wrist for the hair tie I kept there but came up empty. Sighing, I returned to staring out at the dark landscape, not really taking in any of the details. There was too much rushing through my mind for me to focus on anything else.

From almost being kidnapped again, the message from Blackhawk, and the invitation to join the Order, I was overloaded.

Knowing there was only one person I wanted to talk to, I pulled out my phone and dialed my best friend.

"Fin! Oh my goodness, it's so good to hear from you. I've missed you so much. I know we just talked the other day, but I was angry then. How are you?

How are you doing with Cohen and Asa?" she rushed out in her typical Sawyer way.

Laughing, I wiped a tear that had escaped, already feeling better from just hearing her voice. "Slow down, Sawyer."

"Oh, no. I know that voice. What happened?"

Sitting down in a chair, I spilled everything to her, not holding any details back this time. I was tired of limiting myself. It was time I let people help me. I sat back, a big breath leaving me when I was done.

"Wow, I didn't realize how good it would feel to say all that."

"Girl! It's about time you did. I can't believe you've been dealing with all of this on your own. I'm glad you finally trusted me enough to share."

Remorse filled me as I heard the pain in her voice. "No, Sawyer, it wasn't about trusting you. It was about trusting myself to not have to control everything. Ugh, I think I should start seeing my therapist again. I hadn't realized how much I'd been carrying around, trying to manage it all on my own. And now, I'm in this mess."

"Which sounds kind of cool. From what Isla told me, this Order is legit. They don't ask just anyone. It was their creed that saved me with the Council."

"Yeah, I forgot about that. That actually makes me

feel a little better. But… what about Cohen working for them?"

"So? He never lied, and it wasn't like he was spying on *you*. And it sounds like there were serious consequences if he said anything. You can focus on that, or you can give him the benefit of the doubt. I think he's earned it."

"You make it sound so simple." I sighed, rubbing my head.

"If I learned anything in the past year, the things you want your life to be based around are simple. Grab hold of those you love and follow your heart. You might get hurt, but the journey is usually worth it. Henry and I wouldn't have another chance at the Olympics if we hadn't taken the risk."

"Wait, what?" I shrieked, standing up and almost dropping my phone.

"You didn't know?" she asked, her voice small, making me realize just how much I was hurting those I loved.

"I'm sorry. I've been a shit friend. Tell me all about it."

Listening to Sawyer tell me about her show and how the rest of our friends and family had shown up to be there made me miss her more. I was happy for her and my brother. But as the sinking feeling of not being accepted started to filter through, I knew I had to finish what I'd come to do. I just needed to go about it differently.

"I miss you so much," I said, not hiding that I was wiping the tears. "I promise to not run away or keep things from you ever again. Can you forgive me?"

"Of course, Fin. You're my sister. I love you. And if anyone understands what it means to fight a battle from the past, it's me. Just remember that it works better with others." I heard some ruffling and mumbling, and it sounded like Sawyer had placed her hand over the receiver. "Sorry, there's someone who wants to talk to you," she huffed before handing the phone over.

"Fin," Rhett grunted, and I knew I was in trouble.

"Hey…" I cringed even though he couldn't see me.

"Don't 'hey' me. Tell me that you're done being a martyr and that you will let people help you."

"I promise. Cohen, Milo, and Asa are here. Even if I wanted to run away, they'd find me. Heck, I'm pretty sure Milo has placed a tracker on me already," I grumbled, rubbing my forehead.

"Good," he huffed, a pleased tone to his voice. "I gave you a pass last year, but not anymore. You hurt Sawyer, and I won't let you do that again."

"I know. And you're right. It was selfish of me. I was just in such a dark place, it felt like the only way out. Can you forgive me? I'm sorry I left on your birthday and used that as an excuse to sneak away. I'm the worst friend, and I promise to make it up to you when I'm back."

"You better. I think a chick-flick marathon is in order."

I smiled, my shoulders dropping. Rhett might seem like an oversized bear to most people, grumbling at them to get out of his way, but he was a true romantic at heart and had been my movie-watching companion for a few years.

"You bet. Thanks for caring and looking out for Sawyer. I'm glad she has you."

"Hmph, well, I'm glad to have her. We both need you too. You're our friend. Don't forget what that means to someone like me."

Nodding, I realized he couldn't see me. "Yeah, you're right. Is Henry around?" I asked, knowing I needed to talk to him too.

"No, he's out with Soren. They went to hear Shadows of Mayhem. I think Henry might write a song for them."

"Wow! That's so cool, I didn't realize they'd contacted one another. Shit. Okay, I feel like I'm missing so much. Maybe I should just come home?" I bit my lip, knowing Rhett wouldn't spare my feelings from the truth.

"Take care of what you need to, Fin. Everything will still be here when you return. But if you don't deal with it, you'll just find yourself back to where you are now, missing out on everything. So, it's better to handle it now."

Taking a deep breath, I accepted what he had to say. "You're wise, Rhett Taylor. Can I say goodbye to Sawyer?"

"Be safe, Fin," he grunted.

"I will." Smiling, knowing that was his way of saying he cared.

I waited until my bestie returned, already feeling lighter from talking to them both. Once we said our goodbyes and I promised to check in every few days, we hung up. Leaning my head back against the chair rest, I took a deep breath and then exhaled, the stress falling away as the air left my body.

"How's my sister?"

Jumping, I peeked over my shoulder, finding Asa leaning against the glass door. I hadn't realized he'd come outside. Blushing, I hoped he couldn't see it and hadn't heard all the boy drama I'd spilled to Sawyer.

"Um, good. She's excited about qualifying for nationals. One step closer to the Olympics now."

Asa smiled, pride showing for his sister. "Yeah, did you see it?"

I shook my head, dropping my eyes. "No, I, uh, forgot." I began to fidget with the chair, picking at nothing just to distract myself.

"Hey, don't do that. I know you would've been right there if you could've. So do Sawyer and your brother. Let's just focus on doing what we need to do to return home. Okay?"

Glancing up, I found him watching me, nothing but love and warmth on his face. "Yeah, that sounds good. Um, do we have any more information? Sorry I just left. I kind of needed some air."

Asa walked in front of me, leaning against the balcony, facing me. "Yeah, Cohen spoke with his handler, and they've arranged for us all to be allowed to accompany you."

"Really?" I raised an eyebrow in question, wondering how that happened.

Asa chuckled, grabbing my hand. "Cohen said we were all going to be there anyway, so they might as well put Milo and me to work."

Smiling, I linked our fingers, raising our hands to peer at it. "So, Milo, too?"

"Yeah. He doesn't start at his residency until late summer, so he has some time off."

"And," I swallowed, dropping my eyes, "what do you think about him?"

"I think the better question is, what do you think about him? Or *feel* for him?"

Blowing out a breath, I lifted my eyes, knowing I needed to be looking at him when I talked about my feelings. "I like him. I was too afraid to admit it, but I do."

Asa kneeled down, placing both of his hands on my thighs. "Have I given you the idea that I wouldn't be open to the type of relationship my sister has? If I have, I'm sorry for making it where you couldn't talk to me."

Instantly, shame filled me, and I moved forward, taking his face into my hands. "Oh, Asa, no. I'm sorry you thought that for even a second. You've been the best boyfriend, hands down. I didn't think I deserved to be selfish and ask for myself. It was all me. Since I was a teenager, I've hated parts of myself, and I've tried to change, hide, or omit them so others would like me. It's my insecurity, and I'm sorry it leaked out onto you."

"Don't you get it, Fin? I'm not perfect. You act like I am, but I'm just as insecure, selfish, and cowardly as the next person. I knew you were struggling, but I didn't want to push you, afraid I'd lose you completely, so I let you be. I should've tried harder. Maybe then you wouldn't have felt you had to run away. I'm sorry."

"Ssh, you have nothing to be sorry about. Asa, babe, you're amazing. Even if you don't see yourself as perfect, you are to me. I love you so much. I'm sorry I made you doubt yourself. Can we promise to talk to one another about everything, even if it's uncomfortable?"

"I like the sound of that." He leaned forward, kissing me briefly. "And as far as the other two guys go. I know you have a connection with them both. I can see it when you're with them. I'm cool with Milo too. If you find you want to explore things, I'm not going to run away screaming. I'm here to stay, Finley. I waited a whole year just to ask you out. I'm not going to run off scared now that I got you."

"You really are the sweetest," I said, kissing him again. Wrapping my arms around his neck, I pulled him to me, needing his hug. Asa came willingly, and we held one another for a while, just content to be near each other.

When his hands started to roam, I couldn't deny that my lady parts were heating up. Lifting my head, I boldly watched him as he unbuttoned my shirt. Since he was still on his knees, I could see every move he made as his jaw tensed, his nostrils flared, and his pupils blew.

"Are you sure?" he asked, his hand wavering in the air between us.

"Yes. We'll just have to be quiet. But we're high enough up here that I don't think anyone would be able to see us."

"I kind of like the thought that they could." Asa grinned, showing me a whole new side to himself.

Dropping my shoulders down, the shirt slid off, leaving me only in my bra. Slowly, I reached forward, unsnapping the front clasp, glad I'd decided to wear this one today. As soon as my breasts were displayed, my nipples pebbled from the breeze, drawing Asa's eyes to them. He licked his lips, and I knew he was a second away from striking.

Reaching down, I unbuttoned my shorts, the movement snapping him out of his staring contest with my tits. Asa jumped up, pulling his clothes off in quick succession as I pushed my shorts and panties to the ground. At this angle, his cock jutted out at eye level as it began to harden right in front of me, rising up like it was saying hello. Leaning forward, I lifted my eyes to watch Asa as I kissed the tip.

He sucked in a breath, hissing as my warm tongue swirled around it. I moved to take more of him into my mouth when his hands shot out, lifting me under my armpits.

"I don't think I can wait tonight. I need you, Fin."

Sucking in a breath at the desire in his voice, I

barely nodded before I was spun around, and my hands caught the railing I'd been standing against earlier. Asa's hands skated down my body, leaving a trail of goosebumps in their wake. The cold air kissed my skin as I breathed in anticipation of what would come next.

Tilting my head back, he bent down to kiss me, his tongue swirling with mine in a passionate embrace. His hands trailed over my breasts, pinching and teasing the mounds as he explored my body. The world around us ceased to exist as he mapped out my body with his touch.

"More," I gasped, breaking the kiss to state my claim. A sound similar to a growl left his lips as he pulled my hips closer to him, his hard cock nesting between my ass cheeks. His fingers lowered to my pussy, finding me warm and waiting for him.

He began to lightly touch my clit, giving me only teasing caresses as I pushed forward, wanting more friction. A frustrated sigh left me as he kept moving his fingers away each time I tried.

"Asa," I begged, hoping he'd take mercy on me.

His head bent, nipping lightly on my neck as he whispered in my ear. "I like it when you say my name so full of need."

Before I could respond, he gave me what I

wanted, plunging his fingers into me and making my knees buckle as they filled me.

Biting my lip, I barely contained the moan that wanted to escape. Pushing against the railing, I rubbed against his cock, no longer satisfied with his fingers. Spreading my legs wider, I arched my back, hoping my core would be closer so he could slip in.

Asa chuckled, taking the sign for what it was, and moved his hand, positioning it on my hip as he tilted me the rest of the way. I helped him move into the right spot by going up on my tiptoes. As he slipped into me, I let go of everything I'd been holding, allowing it to escape into the night air around me, my moan becoming one with the breeze.

Together, we found a rhythm as he plunged his hard length into me, easily sliding in and out. The sounds of skin slapped against one another, adding to the night sounds. Little gasps and puffs of air were all that could be heard as we let our desire take over.

"I can't last much longer," he groaned, and I nodded, needing him to tip me over the edge.

"I'm ready."

"Fuck, I didn't put on a condom," Asa groaned, stopping his movement.

"Don't you dare stop, Asa! We're good. You know we are."

A little chuckle left his lips before he bent and kissed the dip between my neck and shoulder. His fingers tightening on my hips was the only warning I got before he plunged back into me, pushing a gasp from me. One hand moved around to the front, finding my clit, and he rubbed in circles as he pistoned in and out. It was all I needed before I felt my body tensing up and everything exploded as I came.

My head dropped back, and he sealed his lips to mine, stealing the moan from my mouth. A few seconds later, he stuttered as his hips slammed into me one last time, and he held himself tightly to me as he jerked inside. Pulling our lips apart, we stared at one another in the darkness, and I knew that every-thing he'd said was true. There weren't any more secrets between us, and I looked at him for the first time as my true self.

"I love you," I whispered, needing to put it out into the world, adding to the sounds of our love in the night.

"I love you." He smiled, pecking my lips before he slowly pulled out. My calves screamed at me from the position as I lowered back to the ground.

"You ready to face them?" he asked as he picked up our clothes, handing me mine first.

"Yeah. Plus, I'm starting to get cold, and if we

stay out here much longer, I doubt we'll get away with what we did."

"It's cute you think we did."

Laughing, I got dressed and found Asa holding out his hand for me when I was done. Placing mine in his, we walked into the hotel room together, ready to face our next adventure.

We found Milo asleep on the bed, while Cohen busily worked on his laptop. He looked up at our entrance, closing the lid and moving around the bed toward us. He stopped in front of me, worry etched on his brow as he searched my eyes for something.

"I promise, there aren't any other secrets. I told my handler that I wouldn't keep anything from you anymore. He agreed as long as I can get you to come to the Order and see it for yourself before you make up your mind."

"Okay," I said, stopping whatever speech he had planned.

"Wait, you're not going to fight me on this?" His brow arched up as he looked between Asa and I.

"No. I'll see what they have to say. If they can help, then I'm willing to listen. Did you discover anything on the IP address?"

"It's running through a program that's looking for all possibilities. I'm beginning to wonder though if maybe it's not an IP address but a location of a server."

"What makes you think that?" I asked, just as I yawned. "You know what, never mind. Let's get some sleep. I'm tired. We can discuss it in the morning. There's been a lot to unpack today,"

"Seems like you unpacked something on the balcony," he teased and I rolled my eyes, trying to hide the blush.

Walking into the bathroom, I quickly washed my face, peed, and cleaned myself up before I got ready for bed, changing my clothes. When I found both Asa and Cohen standing at the foot of the bed when I emerged, I wasn't sure what the problem was.

"Everything okay?" I asked, adjusting my glasses.

"Yeah, it's just..." Asa pointed toward the bed, and I realized that Milo had spread out in our absence. "He looks so peaceful. How do we tell him to move?"

Giggling, I walked over and took Milo's glasses, which had gone crooked in his sleep. Brushing his hair over, I waited for him to wake up.

He blinked slowly, looking at me with adoration I didn't feel I deserved, but Sawyer's words to embrace the affection and let the guys tell me how they felt helped me not dismiss it.

"You want to change into something more

comfortable? I'm sure the guys can give you something." I peeked over my shoulder, finding Asa already holding out a pair of sweats and a shirt. Taking it from him, I placed it on Milo's chest. His hands clasped onto mine, holding them for a second.

"Did you decide what you're going to do?" he asked as he began to sit up. I went to hand him his glasses but stopped when he started to untie his bowtie and unbutton his shirt. When I didn't say anything, he stopped, looking up at me. I didn't know how good his vision was without his glasses, so I tried to school my features to make it less obvious I was checking him out.

"Hm?" I asked, the guys chuckling behind me. I'd somehow forgotten that even though Milo might not be able to see me, Asa and Cohen could. "Oh, right, yes, I guess we're all going in the morning."

"Me too?" he asked.

"Yes, I'd like for you to if you wanted. Asa said you had some time off?"

"I do. I just didn't want to assume."

"Oh, well, yes, mmhmm." After confirming him joining us, Milo continued undressing, stripping down to his boxers.

"Is this okay?" he asked, looking around the room. "I usually sleep naked, but I figured that wouldn't be appreciated."

"Speak for yourself," Cohen mumbled, making me smile.

"Yeah, it's um, fine with me," I said, a little too brightly. "You okay to share with us? It might be a tight squeeze."

"I bet it is," Cohen whispered, making my cheeks red. I couldn't take his commentary any longer, so I turned, narrowing my eyes at him. He played it off, whistling like he hadn't been saying anything.

Setting the clothes Asa had given me on the table, I looked between the three guys, trying to figure out what order. "Um, anyone okay with being guy to guy? What do we do, butts to butts? Feet to head?"

Asa chuckled, stepping forward and putting me out of my rambling misery. "I'll sleep at the end. You can be the middle. I already got my cream," he whispered before kissing my forehead, and plopping down at the foot of the bed. Cohen tossed him a pillow, and he shoved it under his head, crossing his feet over one another, looking completely relaxed.

Sighing, I turned back to the guys. Cohen had taken Asa's decision as his cue to slide into the other side of the bed, leaving me to climb over one of them. Milo saw my dilemma, making me think he must've noticed my ogling of him, and picked me up, placing me in the middle.

Everyone settled down, the room going dark as

Cohen turned out the light. Breathing could be heard as everything quieted, the sounds of three people making me hyperaware of every move I made. Eventually, I was able to fall asleep, and I wondered if I'd wake up with something poking me in the back again.

Though, I couldn't say I minded how that had ended.

UNCONSCIOUSLY, I worried things would be weird when I woke, but surprisingly they were so normal that I was beginning to wonder if I'd woken up in a different life. The guys had all seemed to bond and were working together better than some pit crews. Breakfast this morning had been an enormous spread they'd managed to put together, and now they were dividing the tasks for the day before we left like soccer moms before a tournament.

It was scary how sexy I found their organization and team spirit. Hopefully, they remembered to get me some new underwear, or I was doomed.

When Cohen brushed against my leg for the third time, I could no longer take it, and I gasped as I shifted.

"Yes, sweetheart?" he asked, his fingers trailing up my leg.

"I didn't know my legs were a keyboard," I hissed when his fingers got to the hem of the oversized t-shirt I was wearing. I'd gambled that I'd be okay for a few hours while I waited for Asa and Milo to return with clean clothes. It seemed like Cohen would cash in on that bet and tease me until I caved.

The joke was on him. I was a horrible gambler and always folded. I was practically putty in his hands if he dared to take it.

Looking up at him, I found him closer than I remembered as he hovered over me, his stubble brushing against my cheek. His stormy blue eyes bore into me with such an intensity that I forgot to breathe.

He didn't waste words asking, descending down onto my lips like it was the most natural thing for us. And perhaps for us, it was. Cohen was the boy I'd known in a different form for over five years now. Kissing him felt like the answer to all the nights I'd wondered if a boy would ever notice me.

The laptop was moved from Cohen's lap, and I quickly replaced it as he shifted me. Straddling him, I brought my hands to his hair, weaving them into the tresses. He groaned beneath me as I began to rock into him. When Cohen's hands dropped down to my shirt, and he began to lift it, I pulled back, biting my lip as I watched him. Raising my arms, I dared him with my eyes to proceed.

Smirking, he pulled the shirt over my head and then stared, his eyes wide. "Fuck, sweetheart. You've been sitting next to me all morning practically naked?"

Lifting a shoulder up, I smiled. "I like to live on the dangerous side."

Cohen coughed on my words as he began to grow harder beneath me. "How dangerous do you feel like being today?" he asked, skimming his finger over the top of my breast. His eyes dropped, watching his finger as it dipped and lowered around the other.

Reaching down, I unzipped his pants as I watched him. When my hand grazed the waistband of his boxers, his eyes jumped to mine, no longer focused on my breasts. "Very," I said, tucking my fingers under the elastic band. Coarse hair greeted me as I lowered my hand, finding his hard cock waiting for me.

Stroking it, I gripped it firmly in my grasp as he sucked in a breath, waiting to see what I would do next. Pulling his boxers lower, I freed him. It was kind of hot being completely naked with Cohen still dressed, only his cock out on display.

Taking his dick into my hand again, I rolled it

around as I looked at it closely. It was girthy, and I hoped I'd be able to take it. Licking my lips, I debated bending over and kissing it.

"If you do that, I'll be a goner," he rasped, his voice hoarse.

Peering up at him from under my eyelashes, I decided to do as I said and live a little dangerously. Lifting up on my knees, I gripped his cock with one hand as I positioned him at my entrance.

"Shit," he mumbled, his body tensing as he waited for me to move. I could see how much he was holding back, giving me this moment to own. It seemed Cohen knew me better than I'd ever imagined.

"Are you sure you're ready?" he asked, giving me one last out.

Nodding, I leaned forward, kissing him as I slowly lowered myself onto him. His thick cock stretched me more than I'd ever been, and I sucked in a breath as he continued filling me. When I was fully seated, I pulled back, taking in a breath. Cohen's eyes drilled into me, begging me to move.

Rising up, I quickly slammed myself back down, hoping if I did it quicker, I'd adjust faster. Gasping, I held onto his shoulders as he cursed. I could feel parts of his zipper biting into my bare backside, giving me a reprieve from the feeling of him filling me up.

"You're doing so good, Fin. Do you want help?"

I started to nod just as we heard a beep at the door. Eyes wide, I stared at Cohen for half a second before he was lifting me off him and pulled my shirt over my head. Quickly, I tucked it under me just as he pulled the laptop into his lap when the door opened. His pants were still undone, but the computer covered them for now.

Our breathing was quick, so I focused on the screen as I tried to calm my racing heart. Was what we did wrong? Was he having second thoughts?

"Stop whatever you're thinking. I just panicked about being found in a compromising position, not about the act itself," he whispered just as Asa walked into view.

"Clothes have been dropped off. They'll bring them up when they're clean. In the meantime, I got you a few things," Asa announced, smiling at us. I peeked up and discovered Asa standing with a few bags. I looked behind him to see if Milo had returned, but found it empty.

"He had one more stop to make and wanted to do it on his own," he said in answer to my look. Nodding, I focused back on the bags in his hands, trying to ignore the slickness between my legs as giddiness filled me at the prospect of new clothes. Rubbing my hands together, I started to bounce at what lay inside them.

"Damn, if that's the response clothes get, I want to buy them next time. Go on, give us a show," Cohen said, chuckling as he nudged me toward Asa, a slight dare in his voice.

Glancing at him, I raised my eyebrow as we stared at one another, seeing who'd cave first. This time, I had a feeling I'd win. With a squeal, I hopped up on my knees, clapping as I smiled at the pretty things. With a wink, I began to crawl forward, knowing full well that my pussy, which had to be glistening at this point, would be on full display for Cohen.

A curse and a shift of the laptop had me smirking as I snatched the bag and dumped it onto the bed, finding a few tops, jeans, and best of all, some underwear and a bra. I fingered all the items, the thrill of new things making me high as I began sorting the clothes into outfits while keeping my butt lifted, so Cohen had to stare at it.

"Thank you," I said, jumping up to kiss Asa. Wrapping my arms around his neck, the earlier heat returned, and I got the idea to see how far I could push our newfound relationship. Nipping his ear, I leaned forward to whisper.

"Were you serious about seeing where this leads us?"

He pulled back, looking me in the eyes. "Yes. I'm not scared. Why?" he whispered, never dropping his green orbs from mine.

I peered over my shoulder and saw the pure need on Cohen's face, the want still present. It seemed we were all going to find out if we were okay with everything we'd said.

"You should check out what Cohen and I got up to while you were gone."

"Okay," Asa said, looking over my shoulder. Taking his hand, I pushed it under the shirt and onto my pussy. His eyes widened as he looked back at me, a grin spreading across his face. "It seems I interrupted something." His fingers began to tease my labia, and I felt a body press into me from behind. "How can I help?" Asa asked, but it was clear it wasn't to me, but Cohen.

"I think Fin's done enough talking for today. Maybe you can give her something to occupy her mouth?"

Cohen's warm hands landed on my ass as he pushed the shirt over my head. I sucked in a breath as it was removed for the second time. Asa's eyes widened as he nodded enthusiastically. He grabbed the shirt I'd been wearing from Cohen and tossed it, unhooking his pants as he watched Cohen fondle my naked body.

His hands gripped my hips, and I felt his cock slide between my legs, rubbing against my pussy. With a moan, I lowered onto my elbows, lifting my ass higher for him to enter me. Cohen didn't hesitate, pulling me onto him in one go, my garbled scream lost in the bed as my head fell forward at the force.

"Holy fuck, Batman!" I shouted as he began to thrust into me, no longer taking it slow but showing me just how good it could feel as he plunged deep.

Lifting my head, I found Asa stroking himself as he watched the show before him. It was hotter than I imagined seeing him get off on me being impaled by another man.

"Don't forget your role, Asa. Stuff her mouth," Cohen growled, reaching down to pinch my nipple with one hand. Moaning, I opened my mouth as he stepped forward, ready to take him. It was odd at first, as Cohen's thrusts pushed me further onto Asa's dick, but I soon lost track of what was happening when my body began to race toward an orgasm. I'd never come this quickly before, and the knowledge of that scared and excited me.

Asa held my head in his hands as he used the momentum of Cohen to fuck my mouth. Looking up, I checked again, worried I'd find him mortified by what he was participating in, but as usual, Asa surprised me. Nothing but love and lust stared back at me as he peered down. The last of my resolve fled, and I allowed myself to let go and throw the worrying out the window. I toppled over as soon as I did, my body following behind my mind as waves of pleasure crashed into me.

Body spasming, I closed my eyes as what felt like a million white stars exploded around me. With a grunt, I felt Cohen tighten his grip on me as he thrust harder, holding me to him. I moaned, the vibration being all Asa needed as he erupted down my throat. Swallowing him down, I panted when he removed his cock from my lips, my body no longer able to hold itself up; my muscles had turned to jelly.

The guys laughed as I fell onto the pile of clothes, feeling completely at ease being naked. Asa scooped me up a few minutes later and walked me into the bathroom. With great care, he washed me off in the shower, paying extra attention to my hair. Each gentle caress made me love him even more.

"Thank you," I whispered later as he draped a towel around me.

"You don't have to thank me, but you're welcome."

"It's more than just the shower. You take care of me in a way I've never been taken care of before. I didn't even know I desired that, so thank you. You haven't once admonished me for caring about more than one guy, and even though this revenge quest has nothing to do with you, you're here, supporting my crazy mission. So, thank you. I love you, Asa."

"I hope you realize one day that you don't have to thank me for those things, Fin. I love you. Your crazy is my crazy. I'm not going anywhere." Kissing my lips, I had to stop myself from melting into a pool of goo.

"Now, I believe we're owed a fashion show," he teased, waggling his eyebrows. Grinning, I raced out into the room, grabbing the new things he'd bought me. Cohen laughed but set the computer aside, eager for the show, apparently.

That was how Milo found us a few minutes later as I pretended to walk the catwalk in a pair of black jeans, a scoop neck top, and my boots. He grinned as he walked in, placing his bags down onto the dresser and waiting until I was finished to tell us what was in the bags.

"So?" I asked, no longer able to wait. He smirked, looking over at Cohen.

"Well, Cohen and I thought it would be a good idea for us all to be connected. So, I got us some smartwatches, and he's going to program them so we can always find one another no matter where we go.

It only works if we wear them, but it's better than nothing."

"You did that for me?" I asked, looking between Cohen and Milo.

"Of course, sweetheart. I trust the Order, but it doesn't mean there's not something going on where we're worried about your safety. I've programmed a lot of cool features where you can reach out to any of us and let us know if you're in trouble, need help, etc."

We spent the rest of the night going over the tech, and like the nerd I was, I couldn't wait to play around with it. Before too long, it was time to pack and get some sleep before we started on our long journey. I hadn't expected my mission to turn out this way, but as I smiled into my pillow, I knew I was glad. Now, if I could only figure out what Blackhawk's message meant.

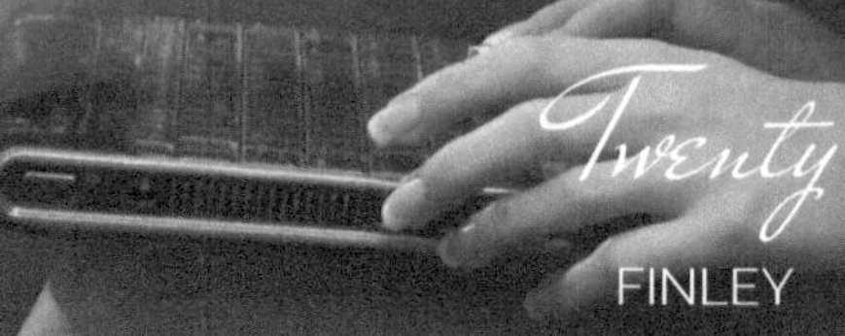

AFTER SPENDING A DAY TRAVELING, I was wiped and ready to crash onto the nearest soft surface. It had nothing to do with the increase in my sex life. Nope.

We'd only gotten a few hours of sleep before the alarm went off, spurring us all into motion as we got ready. First up had been a flight on a private plane, which was my new favorite way to fly, taking us up north. From there, it was a three-hour drive by car through mountains, firmly making it my least favorite way to travel. I'd be happy if I never saw a sign for a switchback curve again.

When we all finally stepped out of the SUV, I didn't know who was happier to have it over with. We all looked a little green around the edges from motion sickness, except for Cohen, who'd been driving and seemed to take delight in our plight.

"Come on, I'm famished," he said, patting his stomach. The thought of food had me clutching my stomach again as nausea rolled through me.

"Yeah, pass."

Cohen chuckled, walking toward me. "Come on, sweetheart."

He took my hand, leading me toward the ominous-looking building. Though, if I imagined a secret facility for a place, this wasn't exactly what I had envisioned. It was concrete and looked like a place people went to die a slow death as a taxidermist or something.

Asa and Milo trailed behind us, both quiet as well. I didn't know if we were all nervous, nauseous, or just plain tired, but the conversation had been at a minimum all day as we'd traveled. I'd been sucked into my own thoughts, so I wouldn't focus on all the varying reasons why no one was speaking. Nope, I wasn't going to spiral in a million directions. I wasn't going to do it.

"You ready?" Cohen asked, breaking my cycle of thoughts.

"Yeah." I glanced over my shoulder, finding Asa and Milo nodding.

Cohen squeezed my hand and knocked on the

door. A screen appeared, surprising me. But when I really thought about it, it shouldn't have. If this place was as high-tech as I expected, they would have the most advanced technology.

Cohen's face was scanned, and then he placed his hand on the pad. Once he was done, he turned, looking at all of us. "You'll need to scan as well. Biometrics of everyone in the building are recorded for safety precautions."

Nodding, I stepped up, the screen flashing over my face. I could feel the warmth of the laser as it scanned, and I hoped it wasn't exposing me to radiation or anything. Once it beeped, an outline of a hand popped up, and I placed mine over the screen. Once it was done, my name appeared with my date of birth on the screen.

Stepping back, I made room for Asa and Milo to go through the process. Once the four of us had passed, the door beeped louder, a hissing sound emerging as it opened.

"Was that sealed?" I asked, and Cohen looked at me, nodding. He had a smile on his face I hadn't seen before, and I could tell he was happy to be here.

"Yeah. Security is top-notch. All the tech here is absurd. I can't wait to show you some of it. Come on." Again, he grabbed my hand, pulling me over the threshold. Excitement vibrated through his whole body. I wondered if he'd been electrocuted for a second.

The interior didn't match what I expected, either. It was a stainless steel room with no personal effects. There wasn't a desk or any furniture. Just an elevator bay at the back. Cohen walked toward it, and I peeked over my shoulder at the other two. They were both looking around as I had, looks of confusion plastered on their faces. Asa caught me watching and raised his shoulders.

The elevator opened as we approached, and we stepped in. There weren't any buttons to push, so it was a little unnerving when the doors shut and it began to move. Cohen watched me, a smile on his lips. Scrunching up my face, I gave up, trying to figure it out, and sighed.

"How?"

With a short laugh, he pointed to the camera in the elevator's corner. "Someone is watching and knows where people are meant to be. It will only go to the floor you're authorized to be on at a specific time."

"Phew, I was beginning to think it was a magic elevator or something," Milo said, blushing.

"I mean, it kind of is," Asa replied. "Who's to say tech isn't magic in some form?" He shrugged his shoulders, completely serious.

"You're a nerd," I gasped, slapping his muscular arm. "I never realized it because you hide it so well. But under all the brawn and goldness is a bona fide nerd!"

This time, it was Asa's turn to blush as he shrugged his shoulders, not responding. The elevator began to slow, and we all stopped talking, unsure of what to expect when the doors opened. So far, it had been sterile, quiet, and devoid of people. I couldn't imagine an entire order being that way. There had to be people somewhere, right?

The elevator stopped, and I sucked in a breath as I waited. It felt like forever, but the doors began to open, revealing what lay beyond. Noise greeted us as it opened into what appeared to be a common room. It was so different from upstairs that I almost felt like I'd stepped off into a different world. Maybe the elevator *was* magic after all, because I definitely felt like an outsider stepping into this setting.

People stopped talking when they heard the elevator, and they turned to look at us. Cohen exited first and was greeted with a loud welcome as people began to converge on him. I stayed back with Asa and Milo as we watched it unfold.

"Is it me, or does it seem like he's really popular here?" Milo whispered.

"No, I agree. I mean, he's a friendly guy, that's not

the weird part, but I never took him as this…" Asa said, waving his hand around.

Nodding, I couldn't help but agree. It was a whole new side of Cohen, but I didn't hate it. He'd always been friendly and outgoing with me online. I hadn't known when we met in person if it was the circumstances or if he was just more reserved face to face. With this new information, I had to guess it was the situation. Or maybe it was the fact he had to keep this part of his life hidden. I knew from experience that when you had to hide something, it began to bleed over into other areas, making you forget what you were hiding to start with after a while.

Cohen seemed to have noticed we'd stopped, turning to reach out a hand for me. I walked forward, waving awkwardly at the crowd.

"Fin, meet some of my old friends. This is Kristina, Asher, and Caleb. We went through training together." A girl and two guys smiled back at me, assessing every part of me, making me feel like I was under a microscope.

"It's nice to meet you all. This is Asa and Milo," I said, wanting the attention off of me, and pointed to the two tall guys behind me. It worked as the trio began to observe the new guys, but I realized my mistake when I caught an interested gleam in Kristina's eyes. "They're mine," I blurted, my face heating. "I mean, with me. Asa's my boyfriend, and um..."

The guys chuckled. I could feel them all shuffling closer, so it didn't seem to make them mad I'd just awkwardly claimed them in front of people without even discussing anything. I didn't even know what we were, but I knew I wanted the chance to figure that out before other people began to make it messier.

Kristina smiled at me, making me feel less awkward. "It's nice to meet you. We haven't gotten to see Cohen in such a long time. I'm glad he was able to return and bring you. He used to talk about you all the time."

I peered up at the man in question, finding him blushing; despite his insistence, he didn't do that.

"Oh, really?" I teased, liking her now that she wasn't drooling all over my men. Fuck, I needed to quit assuming things, but I couldn't deny how nice it sounded and felt to claim them. Sawyer was right again; I needed to stop being scared and take what I wanted.

"Come on, let's show you to your quarters and then grab some food. You must be starving after the trip. It's never fun the first time coming up that mountain," Asher offered, motioning for us to follow.

The other people gathered nodded, saying hello to Cohen and us as we passed. Most of the people were around our age, with a few younger and older mixed throughout. All in all, I'd guess there were about twenty people spread out in the room as we passed through it.

We stopped at a door, and once again, we had to scan our hands to get through it. Cohen hadn't been kidding when he said they had this place wired with biometrics. Stopping at another one about ten down, Cohen placed his hand on the panel and then stepped back.

"Go ahead and scan yours. This door will be set up to allow only us entrance." The three of us nodded, used to the drill now, and scanned our palms. Once that was done, it beeped, and the door opened.

"I'll see you guys in the canteen," Asher said, letting us walk into our quarters. I liked how much they respected privacy here. None of us had brought in our bags, considering we had such few things, so we walked in and looked around, but it didn't take us long to take in the small kitchen, living room, bathroom, and two bedrooms.

"It's nice."

"You haven't seen the best part," Cohen said, grinning. He grabbed my hand, pulling me out of the room and down the hall toward another door. This one didn't require a handprint, so he opened the door, and I was immediately greeted by the smell of detergent and dryer sheets.

"Yes!" I jumped up and down, the excitement coursing through me. "This is my new favorite room." The guys laughed, but I'd gone so long without being able to clean clothes I was desperate for the easy access.

"You can do a load whenever you want. It's free use for all. I know you just did some, but if you need to do anything, our bags should be in our rooms after we eat, once they've gone through checks."

"Oh, I thought we were just waiting, but I guess that makes sense." I shrugged, following them out of the laundry room, a contented sigh leaving me.

"Man, I've never known anyone to get so excited about laundry," Milo whispered to Asa, making him chuckle.

"Fin loves her clothes, and having clean clothes is one of her favorite things."

"I like having all the options laid out for me when deciding what to wear. It's the worst thing in the world when I need a certain top to pull a look together, and it's dirty! The travesty!"

The guys laughed, but I was serious. Fashion

emergencies were no joke. Henry could attest to how many I'd had.

When food smells began to reach us, my stomach growled, no longer angry about all the switchback curves now that I'd settled. The canteen was full of people gathered around tables. It was set up like a restaurant that included a hostess station at the front, tables and booths around it, a bar to the side, and a stage in the back. It was lively, and I loved the energy of the place.

"Wow, this is awesome," Asa said, echoing my thoughts. Cohen smiled that look again, like he'd won the lottery, leading us to the hostess. I finally realized what the look on his face meant. He was home, and he was proud to show it to us, introducing us to people he cared about.

"Cohen! It's been so long. Give me a hug," the woman at the front said, walking around to pull him into an embrace.

"Hey, Grams. I have some people for you to meet." She pulled back, patting his face before turning to us.

"Oh, this must be the lovely Finley I've heard about." She reached out a hand for me, and I grasped it, not realizing she would pull me into her. I went easily, her hugs reminding me of a grandmother I hadn't seen in ages, and her name made sense. She must be the grandmother to all the people here.

"It's nice to meet you."

"It's Karen, but most people call me Grams. Especially after that horrible meme-making my name synonymous with a dumpster fire," she huffed, letting me go.

"Dumpster fire?" Milo whispered, making me laugh.

"Well, I like Grams. I'd be happy to call you that."

"I knew you were the real deal the moment you walked in. I have a knack for that. Now, introduce me to the other two lovely fellas you have here." She lifted an eyebrow, and I had a feeling she knew they were more than just casual acquaintances.

"This is Asa, my boyfriend, and Milo."

They both stepped forward, receiving their own smothering hug. I noticed how Milo melted into her embrace, and I knew I'd need to give him more attention. With what I'd gathered of his family, being part of the Council couldn't have meant they were touchy-feely.

"Welcome to the Canteen. Let me show you to a table." She smiled at us, leading us over to a somewhat private area. It had a wraparound booth that opened to the side of the stage. There wasn't anyone up there yet, just some soft music playing over the speakers. Once we were all seated with me between Asa and Cohen, I looked at him, wondering what we do next.

"So?"

"Someone will be out to ask us what we want in a minute. They usually have two meat options and a vegetarian one each meal."

"Great, I'm starved," Asa said, patting his stomach.

Cohen's phone beeped as someone approached us, and he pulled it out, scrunching up his face. He put it away as the waiter neared, taking over for us.

"Good evening, tonight we have a chicken curry or steak stroganoff. Unless anyone would like to hear the gluten or vegetarian options?" he looked around at us, but we shook our heads. "Excellent. Would you care to start, Miss?"

"Oh, um, sure. I'll have the chicken."

The others went around the table, ordering their food, and we fell into an easy silence as we waited. I didn't know about the guys, but I was busy processing all the new information from the moment we'd stepped out of the SUV. There was a lot to filter through, and my brain was verging on overstimulation.

"Who texted?" Asa asked a few minutes later, reminding me that Cohen had pulled out his phone.

"My handler, he wants to meet."

"Why is that bad?" I asked, noticing the frown on his face.

"In all the years I've been part of the order, I've never met him face to face. Or, well, I might have. You see, everyone here has a code name. Online, we go by those, in person, our real names. We never share our identities to help keep them separate and secret. It also helps build camaraderie. We can form connections with people without feeling competitive with them."

"I don't understand why it's bad then." I reached over, taking his hand.

"Because it goes against everything. So, does that mean I'm no longer going to be part of the Order? Or am I heading into something more dangerous and the information won't matter if I know it because it dies with me?"

The realization of what he said struck me, and I began to look around at everyone, wondering just who they were online. The food arrived, and we all ate in silence, too consumed by what this meant for us to engage in conversation.

Twenty-One

COHEN

WE ALL TRAILED BACK to the room, the earlier excitement of returning to a place that had felt like my only home for years drained with each step. They wouldn't kick me out now, after all this time?

Granted, I hadn't been the best Order agent, but I'd always done my job. Just when it had come to Finley, I'd looked for ways to circumvent the mission. I'd even been shirking them for the past six months, much to my handler's annoyance. When he'd finally told me to approach her, it felt like my life was coming full circle, and I could have the life I'd always wanted.

But what if that was all a lie?

I'd blindly trusted the Order because of who they had been to me, but what if that was childish ignorance coming into play?

"Hey, what if we play some games and not think about death and stalkers for one night?" Fin asked as we stepped into our suite.

"Sounds like a great idea, babe," Asa said, pulling her into his side and kissing her effortlessly on the forehead. It no longer made me envious as I watched their easy affection. She was mine now, and I wouldn't let her go.

"Yeah, there should be some board games in the closet. If not, there will be some out in the common room. We could even see if the others want to join, or just keep it us?" I asked, checking my phone as a message came in. "Actually, our bags are ready. If someone comes with me to grab them, we can look at the games?" I asked, looking up.

"Let's just keep it us. I don't think I can socialize anymore tonight," Fin said, twisting her shirt, and I noticed how tired she did look.

"Of course, sweetheart."

"I'll help," Milo suggested, walking toward the door with me.

"We'll be right back."

Asa and Fin already had the door open to the closet, scrounging through it before we even exited. Laughing, I shook my head as Milo and I fell into a leisurely pace. We were quiet as we made our way to the elevator. I didn't know him as well as Asa, so I debated whether I should wait him out or just lay it all out there. Thankfully, it seemed Milo was ready to talk, making my decision easy.

"Am I dumb for being here? My whole life has been careful decisions laid out to reach a goal that was far away from anything I'd grown up around. I can't say I've been that same guy the last year."

I looked over at him as the elevator moved, assessing what he wasn't saying. "I think the real question is, did you like that person? You said you were tired of being alone, and you can't deny that Fin makes you feel alive in a way only Fin can."

He thought about my words before he slumped against the wall. "Yeah, you're right. I just had a moment of freaking out. I guess I worry I won't have a place with you guys. The three of you already feel so united."

"I understand feeling insecure in your role and place. I do. I've waited years to find it with Fin. The one thing I learned was that you can't stay on the sidelines. If Fin says she wants you here and you want a chance at being a part of her life, then trust that. She's not pulling you along just for fun. That's not who she is."

"Yeah?" he asked, looking at me with hope.

"For sure. Finley is as amazing as you think she

is. It's not an act. Tell her if you want to be part of her life."

"Thanks, I think I will."

The elevator dinged as the doors opened, and I clapped him on the shoulder as I moved out of the space. I turned to the right, knowing where I was headed, and walked toward the surveillance room. Rounding the corner, I froze when I saw who was up ahead. I quickly pulled Milo into the first door that would open. Closing it, I leaned against it, waiting for the footsteps to pass.

"Um, what's that about?" he asked, looking at me quizzically. I realized I was still clutching his shirt in my hands, so I dropped it, smoothing out the material.

"Sorry. Just an old flame I don't want to deal with at the moment."

"Ah, okay. Do you think it's clear now?"

Taking a deep breath, I waited for my heart to slow before peeking my head out the door, looking both ways. When I didn't spot anyone, I nodded, and we both stepped out. We made it to the surveillance room a few more doors down without interruption, making my heart slow the rest of the way.

"Agent Campbell," one of the guards greeted, picking up a clipboard for me to sign. I quickly initialed all of our belongings, scanning them to see if anything had been kept out. It seemed all our items had passed, so I handed the clipboard back to the man.

Milo was looking around at all the computer screens, a look of awe on his face. "This is impressive, and I'm not one who geeks out about this stuff," he said. Laughing at him, I turned to the beeping door as the guard carted our bags out.

"Here you go," he said, returning to the screens. Picking up two, Milo picked up the others, and we made our way back toward the elevator. The corridor was empty, and I sighed, the rest of my body relaxing. Tonight was not the time for an awkward reunion.

The trip back was quiet, both of us consumed in our thoughts, so when the elevator dinged, I jumped slightly. In the common room, Milo followed me over to the bookcase that was overflowing with board games. A few people were still out, playing some, nodding to us in greeting as we passed.

Selecting a few that I liked, I handed one to Milo, and we headed back to our crew. "I'm serious. You should talk to Fin. I thought I could walk away and let her be happy, but I knew I was only lying to myself when I saw her. She's brought me into her life now, and I hate that I waited so long to step forward.

So, if my misery can teach us anything, it's that you shouldn't wait."

Milo nodded, and I placed my hand on the scanner, and we waited for it to beep. When we entered, we found Asa and Fin sitting around a coffee table, snacks and drinks ready for us. They both smiled as we entered, cementing the things I'd said. Asa had become like a brother to me, and I was grateful for his friendship. If I was honest with myself, it was one I hadn't ever let myself have with anyone. I slept around, flitted from city to city, telling myself I wanted it that way. In reality, I was lonely and pining for the type of family I had always wanted.

I had a chance to have everything I dreamed of, and it was right in front of me.

"What did you find?" I asked, looking at the stack of games.

"Connect Four, Sorry, and Monopoly!" Fin cheered, leaning up on her knees to see what we had. She looked so cute in her glasses and short shorts. I was about to suggest another game when I remembered she wasn't there in her relationship with Milo.

Setting the bags down, I placed the games on the table and then took the bags and put them in one of the bedrooms. I pulled out my computer, checking that the Order hadn't placed any new software on it while they had it. After a quick scan, I carried it out to the other room and sat in a chair while they discussed what games to play.

Opening up the program I had running on the code Blackhawk had left us, I found it was still only 40% through all the possibilities. Sighing, I set it aside and focused on the group in front of me.

"What's it going to be, sweetheart?" I asked, focusing on my girl.

"I think we should have a Speed Connect Four tournament, and then maybe a group game?"

"I'm game," Asa said, then laughed at his unintentional joke. Settling down on the couch, I faced off my opponent, who happened to be Fin first.

"No cheating, sweetheart."

"I'd never!" she exclaimed, but smiled, lifting only the corner of her mouth. Laughing, I placed my red piece into a slot, and she followed quickly. Over the next few seconds, we both put tokens into the spaces, trying to find our way to four.

"Ah!" one of the guys said next to us, but I didn't look away, needing to focus on beating Finley. She leaned forward, her shirt dipping a little to show her cleavage. I knew it was a ploy, but like the hungry man I was for her, I fell into her trap willingly and placed my piece without looking.

When she smirked, moving back, I knew she'd won, but I couldn't say I cared anymore.

"I win!" she cheered, giggling.

"No, I'm pretty sure I won, sweetheart." Fin peered up, meeting my eyes, and I watched as she licked her lips, her pupils going wide at my meaning.

"My turn. Championship round," Asa said, interrupting our eye fucking. Milo traded places, and I found the game much easier to concentrate on without Fin as my opponent.

After that, we played Sorry and then finished with a wild game of Uno, where it spit cards at us. I called it when we all started to yawn, knowing that tomorrow would come early.

"Come on, let's go to bed. We should be rested for whatever tomorrow brings."

Everyone nodded, and despite having two rooms, we all ended up in the same bed again, with Milo sleeping at the foot. Cuddling up to Fin, I held her in my arms, happy to be here.

"We'll deal with it together," she said, smoothing her hand over my face. "You taught me that."

Dipping my head down to hers, I breathed her in, feeling my whole being relax. "Thank you for reminding me, sweetheart." Kissing her nose, I snuggled her close, not even caring that Asa's arms were wrapped tight around her from behind.

Dodging an ex, decoding mysterious clues, and facing my handler were all things we'd do together, and I found myself liking the sound of that more and more.

Beeping woke me a few hours later, and I realized the program had found a match. Slipping out of bed, I crept over to the computer and picked it up, the flashing message making me giddy. This was the part I loved. Using my systems and knowledge to crack things, finding the impossible.

I hesitated for a second as I sat in the chair and looked over at Fin sleeping. She looked so peaceful; I hated to wake her. It might be better for me to comb through everything and then condense it for her so she didn't have to sift through all the boring things.

Part of me knew that was a lame excuse, but I carried on, clicking the cursor to follow the program. My earlier guess that it might be more than an IP address turned out to be correct. It was more of a web address to a secret folder. When I typed in the key, it opened, and I found what looked to be conversations. When I saw Blackhawk and Oblivion and another screen name, I paused, the urge to stop filling me, but my need to know what I needed to protect her from overtook my common sense, and I opened it.

Obsidian: It can't be him.

Oblivion: Are you sure? I thought you said

that place was abandoned. How did this happen?

Blackhawk: You both are jumping to conclusions. Mongoose is fine. I promise.

Oblivion: Then who was it? If not him, then who? Do you not care that someone died?

Blackhawk: Of course, I care, little hacker. I'm just saying we're not responsible.

Obsidian: This is messed up. What did you say to him?

Oblivion: Nothing. He just said he needed help. When I asked him what, he returned and said not to worry about it. That he had figured it out and knew how to make things right. I haven't heard from him in days.

Blackhawk: What could going back to the house prove? It doesn't make sense, so the likely reason is that it's not Mongoose.

Oblivion: But what if it is and we do nothing?

Obsidian: Hawk's right. What can we do? We don't know his real name, where he lives or even what he looks like. There's nothing for us to report. If we say anything, we could be seen as accomplices.

Oblivion: But we didn't do anything with this fire.

Obsidian: So, you're just going to say, "Sorry,

officer, we had to break into this place for an illegal hacking club on the dark web and just take a file?" Yeah. He'd lock you up so fast you wouldn't even get to ask for a lawyer.

Oblivion: I don't know if I can just ignore this.

Blackhawk: You have to. As far as MKG is concerned, he left a month ago. We have no connection to him. From this point forward, we don't talk about him. He left our team because of his mistakes that almost cost you Oblivion. We have another mission tonight. I'll take point. You can be security this time, Oblivion. You've earned the break. Do we all agree?

Obsidian: I'm good. You're right. He hasn't talked to any of us. There's no way to know if it's him, so no use concerning ourselves.

Blackhawk: Little hacker?

Oblivion: Yeah, fine. No more thoughts.

Blackhawk: We reconvene in four hours. Be ready.

I clicked on a few more, barely reading them as my mind processed the new information. Fin had briefly mentioned that they'd been a foursome at one point, but she hadn't said why they weren't at the end. Could this be the masked man who had attacked her? Coming back for vengeance after all these years? I skimmed through the messages, but the more flirty they became, the more I felt like I was invading her privacy. Copying all the files onto my own drive, I exited the site with the intention of returning to bed.

Something nagged me during the conversation, though, and I clicked onto one of the secure Order servers of back missions. After an hour of scrolling through files, my eyes closed, and I decided to call it quits. Just as I was about to shut the computer, my cursor moved over a folder, and I blinked, thinking I was reading it wrong.

Magnolia safe house-explosion

Opening the folder, I read the report but found no information that made sense. If it was a safe house, it couldn't have been the same place Fin had broken into. Right?

Crawling back into bed, thoughts plagued me as I tried to put the pieces together. Something wasn't right, and I was determined to figure it out. Fin's life might depend on it.

I WATCHED on the screen as they walked the complex. I'd been watching every single move since they'd arrived yesterday. I was fascinated by them. Every little thing they did made me wonder, and I pondered what it meant. Finley had always been a curiosity of mine, and having her resurface after all these years had me even more desperate to learn as much as I could about her. I hadn't realized how much I'd needed her until she'd disappeared.

Our games had been fun, and I'd gotten back a part of myself I thought had been lost years ago. And after all this time, it seemed like we'd finally be face to face. Nerves filled me, and I didn't know why. I shouldn't be this nervous, but I was. We'd come so close to meeting before, but things were different this time. It wasn't on my terms, but it was necessary.

Someone was trying to hurt her, and I couldn't hide any longer.

When they entered their apartment, I knew it was time. Standing, I smoothed down the black button-down shirt. It wasn't what I usually wore, but it felt like I needed it. Though, paired with my black jeans with holes in the knees and combat boots, I didn't know who I was trying to fool with my shirt. Maybe myself more than I realized.

I'd looked into the other two guys who'd tagged along, needing to know who my competition was. Milo was a descendent of a Council family, but based on what I found, he was clean, never having partici-pated in any of their criminal dealings. I could respect a man who'd bucked family tradition to find his own path. I knew firsthand how difficult it could be to turn away from the sinister side of things. With his recent doctorate and killer fashion sense, I felt intimidated by the man I'd never even met. He had the wealth and prestige to provide a good life for Finley and a respectful career path.

But it was Asa who struck me as the biggest obstacle. While Milo had wealth and an honorable career, Asa was her boyfriend. He was clean-cut, an all-star hockey player, and had connections to her best friend. They'd been dating for almost a year, and

I knew he cared for her. I just wasn't sure how much and whether that could be tested.

Cohen was a surprise for me. I'd known him for years as his handler, a fellow trainee of the Order, and even longer online as Chaos. Our relationship was long and filled with pitfalls that would need to be dealt with. I knew it would be a surprise for him when we came face to face. The secrecy had felt necessary all those years ago, but now I wondered if I hadn't kept it from him for other reasons. Seeing him holding Finley's hand, though, had sent a spike of jealousy through me I hadn't been prepared for.

Knowing I couldn't put this off any longer, I sucked it up and moved toward the door. Walking through the hall, I blanked my face, needing to keep my features neutral amongst the others. Only a select few knew my true role in the Order, and I wanted to keep it that way.

Imperium in Imperio, or the Order as we called it, had been created as a way to bring order to all the agencies around the world. As our founders had known, any time power was involved, it could be easily corrupted, morphing the organism into something it was never meant to be. The Order was there to bring balance back to the fold. And we'd been doing it undercover for decades.

Nodding at a few people, I turned down the hall toward their quarters. This was it. I stopped in front, debating if I should knock or just enter. With my position in the Order, I had access to every room, but I didn't know if I wanted them to know that yet. Letting out a deep breath, I raised my fist and knocked on the door, the chatter inside stopping at the sound.

Footsteps sounded, my trademark smirk crossing my face as I heard the handle turning. A retort to reprimand them for not using the camera crossed my mind, but I held it at bay. This would work better anyway. I wasn't sure if Cohen would open the door if he saw my face.

The former Council heir was the one on the other side, assessing me as he opened it. "Can we help you?" he asked.

I didn't drop my smirk, the role too comfortable to let go of. "I'm here for Finley." It wasn't what I meant to say, but it was true.

His eyes narrowed as he tried to decipher my meaning. Whether or not he took it as the threat it was, was up to him. I would make Finley mine.

"Name?" he asked, not moving, making me respect him.

"Ryker Jenson."

"Don't let him in," a voice said behind Milo, and I peered up to find Cohen staring me down. I looked around him but still didn't see my little hacker anywhere.

"Ah, Cohen, that's no way to greet your *superior*." Cohen's face paled, and Milo looked between the two of us before stepping back and letting me in.

Just as the door closed, the other two walked out of a bedroom with a basket of dirty clothes. "Who was at the door?" Finley asked before stopping and looked up to meet my eyes.

Smirk in place, I waited for her to rush toward me, showing all these guys the bond we had. She dropped the basket, running for me, and I felt like I'd been waiting my whole life for this moment. I opened my arms and waited for her to sweep into them and give me the kiss I'd been dreaming of for five years. When a pain seared me, I blinked, not understanding.

Bending over, I blinked more, looking at my little hacker as tears trailed down my face. Her face was red, and she was breathing hard as she seared me with hatred. I looked up to make sure I'd come to the right place. Asa and Milo looked on in shock, slightly cringing in discomfort. Cohen had a mix of disbelief, fear, and satisfaction at my plight as he stared down at me.

"What the hell, Finley?"

She moved closer, her hands on her hips as she

stared me down. "Don't what the hell me! What are you doing here?"

Cohen moved closer, pulling her further away from me. "Sweetheart, not that I don't appreciate the gesture. But is there a reason why you kicked my *superior*?" he ground out, the word sounding sour to my ears, breaking something in me.

"Your superior?" she asked, shaking her head in disbelief. "No, this is Blackhawk."

At the name, the guys stopped, their faces changing to ones of rage. Backing up, I lifted one hand, still cupping my balls with the other as they throbbed in pain.

"Wait a minute. I think there's a misunderstanding. Yes, I'm Blackhawk, but I'm not the bad guy here."

"That's rich coming from you," Cohen seethed, no longer caring that I was his boss.

"Stop. I think we need to take a minute and talk about things. We're clearly all missing some information."

Finley shook her head, hurt and rage on her face that made me stop, wondering what I'd done to make her look that way.

"I don't understand. Finley, I thought we were playing a game. I didn't mean for you to get hurt.

That's why I called you here. The MKG has grown too big, and we need to stop them."

"MidKnight Guild? They're still out there?" She shook her head, clearing her thoughts. "The only person I have a vendetta against is you. You're the one who ruined my life, and I want my revenge."

I stared, not understanding. But before I could explain, the door to the room opened as three operatives swarmed the space, raising guns at the four of them.

"Halt. Come no closer. Sir, are you okay?" the leader asked.

"Yes, I'm fine. It's a misunderstanding. They're not a threat."

At my directive, they lowered their weapons but didn't exit yet, still waiting for my command as they assessed the situation.

"Sorry, sir, your vitals increased, and we could tell you were in pain. We thought you were under threat. Shall we leave?"

"Yes, I'm fine. Nothing an ice pack won't cure." The three guards nodded, taking their leave.

"Why did they come to your rescue?" Cohen asked, looking at me differently than he ever had before.

Sighing, I closed the door, leaning against it.

"Because I'm not only your handler but the leader of the Order."

Cohen's face paled again as he took in the information. His hand shot out to grab the table, and he slumped down into a chair. The others followed suit, Finley watching me with narrowed eyes. I stayed where I was, predicting the space between us was a good thing for the time being. At least for my balls' sake.

"I think you have some things to explain. First, how about the night you had me arrested?"

She crossed her arms, and I was momentarily distracted by her tits, so when the words sunk in, I stared, sure I'd heard her wrong.

"I'm sorry, what? I haven't gotten anyone arrested."

"Yes, you did!" she screamed, some of her fire emerging, and I reflexively covered my balls, afraid of a second attack.

"I promise you, I did no such thing. Can you please share what you're accusing me of?"

She laughed, the noise appearing off. "Fine. Play it that way. I have nothing to say to you, and if you run this place, I want nothing to do with the Order. This was a mistake."

Fear rushed through me at possibly losing my

chance to finally have Finley in my life. So, I did the only thing I could think of at that moment.

"Well, I'm sorry to hear you feel that way. If you don't want to share what I'm accused of, then maybe a few days to cool off is in order." I smiled at my pun, moving to open the door. Standing in the middle of it, I turned and looked at them. "I'm sorry it's come to this."

Shutting the door, I punched in my code, sealing them inside until I unlocked it again. I heard the knob turn and a scream when it didn't open. Fire filled my veins as I walked back to my office, determined to make Finley talk to me and realize I was the man for her.

THE DOOR SLAMMED CLOSED, and we all stood there, staring. I rushed toward it, twisting it. Screaming, I backed away. My breathing was coming out ragged as I tried to put all the puzzle pieces together.

MKG still existed.

Blackhawk was Cohen's handler.

He wanted me as part of the Order.

The air left me, and I sunk down to the ground, no longer able to keep standing. The memory I'd tried so hard to ignore, the one where everything had culminated, rose to the surface, and I could no longer deny it existed.

If MKG was still operating, what did that mean? Was this Obsidian? Mongoose's ghost? Were they after us? Were any of us safe?

"Fin?" a voice beckoned, but I was too stunned, too overwhelmed, to hear it. The realization that a long-forgotten ghost had emerged had me withdrawing. I couldn't do this. I was too weak to deal with this. It would be better if I just checked out. I didn't deserve love. I wasn't owed anything.

The things I'd done meant I was destined to live a life of solitude, never able to repair the damage I'd caused.

There was no redemption to be found here. I was deluding myself into believing I could. It didn't matter that I'd found Blackhawk. He might've been the one to set me up, but he wasn't the one with blood on his hands. That honor lay only with me.

I'd killed Mongoose, and then conveniently forgot about it to appease my guilt.

"She's in shock. The door's locked. Cohen, can you hack it?"

"Unlikely, if the Order designed it that way, there's no way I'm getting through it."

"Call him back. She needs help. Do it! *Now*!"

The disembodied voices floated around me. I knew the familiar sounds, but it didn't seem to matter. Nothing mattered.

I'd killed someone, and when my family knew, they'd toss me out like I deserved. There was no hope for me. I should've taken that bottle of pills all those years ago. Maybe then I would've saved someone from dying.

Closing my eyes, I let the blackness take me, praying it would all be over soon. There was no redemption for the broken and downtrodden. Happiness and love were a lie I told myself to wake up every morning. But I didn't deserve to wake up.

PANIC SURGED THROUGH ME, and I glanced around, trying to figure out what to do. Everything had spiraled in the last ten minutes, and I felt like someone had hit me in the head with a hockey puck. Milo hovered over Fin where she'd passed out on the floor. Cohen angrily paced back and forth as he tried to reach someone on the phone and I stood there, useless as I tried not to pee my pants.

Fin thought I was perfect, but this was where I failed. I didn't know how to handle things like this. I'd been faced with that realization when she'd been taken, and as she laid on the ground, going into shock, I was hit with it again.

I wasn't enough, and ultimately it was why I realized I needed the other guys. Because at some point, she would've realized it too, and then she would leave.

I was always the one who was left behind.

It had happened since birth when my twin was taken from me. I could feel a part of me missing, and I unconsciously overcompensated for that loss with my parents until finally, I wasn't enough to engage my father's interest, and he abandoned me altogether. My mother was easier to appease, but I could tell she was missing part of her heart. When I found Sawyer, I felt whole again. Everything felt like it was aligning.

But then Fin had been taken, and I realized my flaw.

I wasn't good in a crisis. I couldn't do anything. I had no discernible skills outside of hockey. It was just a waiting game until everyone else figured it out.

The self-defeating thoughts threatened to take over when I looked down at the woman I loved. I would lose her. I would lose them all. Two guys I'd come to feel true friendship with.

Milo and Cohen both said something, looking at me for the answer. My breathing quickened, and I knew I would pass out if I didn't stop it.

"Asa! Snap out of it. This isn't the time to freak out. Fin needs you," Cohen bellowed.

I shook my head, the decision made. "No, I'm just in the way."

Cohen walked over, his own panic evident in his eyes. I waited for him to tell me I was right and that he'd take care of Finley. Dropping my head, I inadvertently placed my face in the path of his fist, and I stumbled back as pain filled me.

The throbbing in my jaw and cheek helped center me, and I peered up, finding Cohen watching me. He shook out his hand, his knuckles red as he watched me. Cracking my jaw, I raised a hand, touching the spot and wincing. The pain filled me, and I held onto it, knowing it was the only thing keeping me from spiraling back into those thoughts.

"Thanks." I nodded, relaxing Cohen, who'd probably wondered if I would retaliate.

"I need your help, don't leave us, man." He stepped forward, squeezing my shoulder and staring me in the eyes. "I know this is fucked up, but whatever demons you're fighting, leave them for now. We'll figure them out later. The woman we both care for is hurting, and right now, that's our focus. She needs all three of us. Maybe... even four. I'm still trying to get my head around the fact that my handler is the leader of the Order *and* Blackhawk, and... well, yeah."

He cleared his throat, and I noticed some of his

own demons surfacing. Cohen was right; we could deal with them later when Finley was awake. Taking a deep breath, I slowed my heart and cleared my head. When I opened my eyes, I found that his eyes were clearer.

"Okay, what can I do?"

"If you can call *Ryker*," he sneered, "and help Milo, I'll keep trying to break through the encryption."

Nodding, he handed me his phone, the five unanswered calls showing. Hitting the dial button, I placed it on speaker and kneeled down toward Milo. He was taking her pulse and muttering under his breath.

"What do you need?"

"What don't I need," he snapped, closing his eyes. He looked up, an apology on his face as his eyes filled with remorse. I didn't need to hear it, though. We were all stressed, so I stopped him.

"It's okay. Better question. What can I do to help you?"

"What?" bellowed over the phone speaker, and we both stopped to stare at it.

"Um, Mr. Ryker?" I asked, picking it up closer. "This is Asa."

"It's just Ryker. Fin ready to tell me?" he asked. I

could almost hear the smug smile he had to be wearing.

"Not exactly, um—"

"Listen, until she's ready to tell me, and we can have a conversation. I have a secret order to run," he interrupted, cutting me off.

"Do you have a medical wing?" Milo blurted, ignoring the man's rudeness. "We need to get her to one before she deprives all of her organs of oxygen and dies. Is that urgent enough for you?" he shouted. It was the first time I'd witnessed the usually calm and collected man irate, and I had to say, I liked it.

"What happened?" Ryker asked as the sounds of his movement echoed through the phone.

"We don't know. She's in shock. Something you said made her go pale, and then she collapsed to the floor, staring off into space. She didn't even know who any of us were before she passed out."

"Fuck, okay, listen, I'm on my way. Tell Cohen the encryption key is 02141995."

I looked up as the phone clicked off and found Cohen nodding that he heard it as he entered it. The door clicked open, and Milo picked up Fin as we hurried out of the room. Turning in both directions, Cohen took off to the left, hopefully leading us to the medical wing. His face was a little ashen, and it helped me not feel so scared, knowing that we all were.

We turned down another hallway, coming to a door, and found Ryker standing in front of it. "Come on," he urged, motioning for us to enter. Medical staff awaited us, taking Finley and quickly hooking her up to monitors. Cohen and I stepped back, letting them do what was needed, but Milo stayed, and I think it helped ease our minds knowing he was there.

When they shut the curtain, we stood with Ryker, whose cocky expression had changed to one of concern. Perhaps he wasn't so bad if he cared for Finley that much.

"Why is MKG bad?" I asked, bringing his eyes to mine. He sighed, looking at Cohen briefly before finding my gaze again.

"I've handled this all wrong. We've gotten off to a wrong start, and I'm not even sure I know what's really going on. I thought Fin and I were playing our games like we used to. It was how we flirted, but it seems like it's something more than that. Why does she hate me?" he asked, looking serious.

"You're Blackhawk, right, from the club she joined to find my sister?"

"Your sister… so she did find her friend then?"

"No, that's a whole other story, they found each other, but that's who you are, yes?"

"Yeah. I went by the name Blackhawk at the time. Why?"

"Well, she hates you because of what you did on that final test."

He blinked, shaking his head. "I don't understand. She messaged the night of the last test, saying she wasn't feeling well, and had gotten grounded, so she couldn't complete it anyway. She stated she'd reapply and go through it again on the next round. But I never heard from Oblivion again after that. Not until a month ago."

Glancing at Cohen, his face held the same disbelief mine did. "Yeah, that's not what happened at all," I said, knowing Fin wouldn't lie about one of the worst nights in her life.

"Denial," Cohen coughed into his hands, though how hard he tried to cover it up was debatable since we both clearly heard it.

"I'm not in denial," Ryker protested, crossing his arms. "That *is* what happened. I waited and waited. I even searched, but no one else had ever heard from her again."

"Yeah, right," Cohen huffed, rolling his eyes.

"What's your problem?" Ryker barked.

"Nothing. It's just not surprising you're lying and think you're so blameless."

Ryker started to argue when Milo stepped out, halting their debate. "She's stable. She'll be okay."

We all sighed in relief, and Milo walked over to take the seat next to me. "And she hates you because you're the reason she was arrested. Just own it, dude," Milo said, closing his eyes as he leaned his head back against the wall.

"What the fuck are you talking about?" Ryker shouted, standing to look at the three of us.

"Fin. She was arrested during the third trial. You set her up," I repeated, narrowing my eyes at the guy. I wouldn't let him dismiss this.

"No, I most certainly *did not*."

"Well, someone's lying. There can't be two versions of the truth, and I believe Fin. Her getting arrested was a turning point for her. She wouldn't lie about it," I said, not backing down.

"And I was there that summer when she did her community service."

"I'm not saying she couldn't have been arrested," Ryker said, waving his hands. "I'm saying I had nothing to do with it."

"Maybe there can be two versions of the truth," Milo said as the rest of us started to argue again.

"How so?" I asked.

"There were other people in your group, right?" Milo asked Ryker.

"Yeah, it was Dex and me with Finley."

"Dex?" Cohen asked, shifting his feet, and I wondered if he knew something he wasn't saying.

"Yeah, he went by Obsidian. We were roommates at the time, but after that year, he transferred schools. He got out of the hacking business, but we're still close friends."

"We need to ask him what his version of the night is then. He might have the missing piece."

"Fine. I don't know what this has to do with anything, but I'll call him. I know what happened, though, and Fin bailed on us."

"That's where you're wrong," a small voice said. We all turned, finding Finley in a wheelchair, an IV attached. The nurse shrugged when we all looked at her.

"She insisted. She's quite convincing."

Smiling, I walked over to her, needing to touch her to know she was okay. "Hey."

She looked up at me, relief in her eyes as she took me in. "Hi, I'm sorry. Everything was just too much."

"I think we all need to have a conversation. A real one," Ryker said, frowning at us.

"Fine," Finley said, sighing. "Can it wait until morning? I'm exhausted."

"Sure. I'll have breakfast sent up and meet you in your rooms."

"You're not going to lock us in again, are you?" Cohen asked, narrowing his eyes.

"No. I won't. Get some sleep. You've had a long couple of days."

The three of us walked back to our rooms, pushing Finley in the wheelchair. We quickly got ready for bed, all of us eager to get some rest after the day.

As I lay there, listening to Finley's breathing, I vowed that I would be there for her no matter what was uncovered. I wasn't going to run away from this. I could be enough for her. She needed the guys and me, and I needed her. Together, we'd fight our demons.

MY HAND TIGHTENED on the stress ball as I squeezed, wishing it was something, or someone, else. Everything I'd planned for years was about to be ruined because one greedy little girl couldn't keep her nose out of my business. I'd have to make sure she got the message this time.

My phone flashed, his number displaying across the screen, and I squeezed harder. I needed to regroup before I spoke to him. I couldn't waste everything now on emotion. When jelly hit me in the face as a handful of beads exploded around me, I looked down, realizing I'd done it again. Another stress ball causality.

My assistant ran into my office with a worried look at the mess. "I'll clean it up, sir."

Scowling, I brushed the gunk off my once pristine

shirt and knocked the squishy balls to the floor. She could deal with it. Standing, I walked over to the closet in the corner of my office and pulled out a shirt, the dry cleaning wrapper still on it. Tossing the soiled one into the hamper, I turned to find my assistant licking her lips as she took in my body.

Rolling my eyes, I ignored her lustful intentions and tore off the plastic before buttoning up the shirt. If she didn't get her daydreams of bedding the billionaire boss in check, I'd have to replace her. It wouldn't be the first time. If someone had told me in high school that the surefire way to get laid was to become a billionaire, I wouldn't have believed them. But here I was, ten years later, and I had more pussy options than I knew what to do with. Especially since pussy wasn't even my thing.

Sitting back at my desk, I clicked on a few windows to see if there had been any new developments. I didn't have time to keep monitoring their progress while putting my plan into place. I'd been this close to succeeding when Finley Reyes decided to get a conscience after all this time.

Pulling up the file of everything I'd gotten away with over the years, my cock started to get hard as I flipped through them. The true aphrodisiac was pulling off criminal actions and getting someone else to do the time. It got me going every time. By this point, I was a pro at it, able to ruin anyone's life with a few keystrokes. The only hurdle was the Order. Otherwise, I would've taken down Finley like I'd done all of my other foes. But she was protected by none other than *him*.

Turning to the framed picture on my desk, I rubbed the hard length in my pants as I stared at it.

"Anything else, sir?" my assistant asked, surprising me.

I turned to her, narrowing my eyes, hoping she'd go away. Instead, she simpered closer, batting her eyelashes.

"I can take care of that for you."

Staring at her, I tried to figure out what she was referring to when she leaned over, her hand outstretched toward my leg. Grasping her wrist, I tightened my grip as she cried out.

"Don't touch me," I seethed, dropping her arm. She fled from the space, giving me the space I'd been wanting. Stupid cunt and her ideas of grandeur.

The phone on my desk beeped, and I picked it up, staring out the window. "What?" I barked, not in the mood to handle any crises.

"The package you wanted has been secured."

Smiling, I felt life begin to surge through me again at the opportunity to make a scene. Yes, this was good.

"Thank you, Miguel. I'll be down shortly."

Picking up the phone, I quickly called HR to let them know I'd need a new assistant and to make sure she signed an NDA before she left.

"Make the next one old. I'm tired of these twenty-something girls trying to come onto me to fulfill some misguided fantasy. I just need someone to do the job and leave me alone."

"Yes, sir. I'll get on it," the voice said, and I hung up, not even caring who I'd just spoken to. The advantage of running your own company, everyone bowed to you and didn't bat an eye at your bad behavior. Though, I'd argue my behavior wasn't bad, just lacking social niceties. There were far too many things for me to conquer to make sure I didn't hurt someone's feelings during it.

Taking the elevator down to the secret floor, I went through the security measures to reach the level that wasn't documented on any blueprints. First, I scanned my hand, followed by a retina scan and then a voice activation.

"Purple tacos," I said, waiting for the screen to light up green. I changed the password daily to a random phrase, so it would be impossible for anyone to predict. My security was some of the best, and in fact, it was what had made me billions.

The elevator lowered and opened to the top-secret

floor, revealing the stainless steel level. The guard at the elevator nodded to me as I stepped off and began my trek toward room #5. My shoes echoed on the floor, bouncing off all the walls with nothing to absorb the sound. It was an easy way to ensure no one could ever sneak up on anyone here if they were lucky enough to make it this far.

I passed the first room, the door shut tight. Each room had a different purpose, and the most sinister were closer to the elevator. Only one other person knew what went on behind that door.

The second door held my latest tech gadgets that I was developing for myself. If you couldn't keep the coolest shit for your own purpose, where was the fun in that? I'd taken on corporations and corrupt men with the things I'd developed, putting me into the position I was currently in today. I could hear the sounds of a saw as I passed, and I made a note to stop by and see their progress before I left.

Behind door three laid a server room that would make any geek jealous. It was how I managed to obtain ownership of MidKnight Guild, ferreting out all the secrets of the creators and, one by one, taking them from them. It had been fun to watch them implode on themselves. And now I ruled it all.

Door number four was perhaps my favorite, but I bypassed it as I came upon number five. It wouldn't do to get transfixed by the things in that room and forget my mission today. No, it would be better to not even peer at it.

The guard at the door nodded in greeting, but I barely paid attention to him. People below me were only good for the role they played. I didn't learn their names, remember their features, or know anything about their lives. It wasn't needed in my line of work, so I shoved all that non-essential stuff to the side and focused on the big picture.

A woman sat in the middle of the room, tied to a chair. She stared at me, not giving anything away as I approached. It seemed the Order taught their agents better than some other organizations I'd taken down.

Leaning against the desk, I watched her, assessing all of her weaknesses before speaking. "You, dear, were very hard to find. I'll give it to the Order for their secrecy. They really do have a knack for fading into the background."

She stared back, not offering anything. It would impress me if I was inclined to be impressed by such things. In my world, time was currency, and she was wasting mine.

"Okay then. If you have nothing to say, you're useless to me." Looking to my left at the guard, I nodded, indicating for him to follow protocol. It was always so fun watching them scramble. "When the gift is ready to send, I have a note to attach."

Saying nothing else, I left the woman alone with the guard, knowing the show was about to start. But as I neared door number four, my eyes drifted toward it, and I couldn't stop myself from walking over. Smoothing my hands over the door, even this part felt more significant than the others. Could a door be sexy?

Placing my thumb on the lock, I waited for the beep before the satisfying hiss of the air locked room emerged. Stepping inside quickly, I blinked a few times as my eyes adjusted to the red light. Wall to ceiling was covered in photos and conversations. Once I'd completed it, no one else had ever been allowed to step foot into this room. It was temperature-controlled and air locked when not in use to not disturb all the images.

Walking over to the couch, I began to strip down as I neared it, knowing I was too weak today to ignore the need coursing through me.

Laying back on the couch that was as old as me, I inhaled the pillow, still able to smell him. I might be a glutton for punishment, but it was one I would willingly accept.

Looking around at the photos, I zeroed in on my favorite as I began to stroke myself. Hitting play on the remote on the table, sounds of his moans I'd recorded filled the room, and it was like I was immersed in him.

His smell. His sounds. His body.

It might not be the real thing, but it was a close second. Quickly, I came, splashing my cum over his face that was plastered to the floor. Smiling, I kneeled down, wiping it over his lips and imagining him taking it.

"Soon, my love, soon."

The story will continue in Lipstick Lies.

How about that ending? I know, I know… another cliffhanger, but good news, Lipstick Lies will be out soon, so you won't have to wait too long to find out the end of Finley's story. If everything goes well, it should be out in September.

I hoped you enjoyed learning more about Finley and the men in her life, and I can't wait for you to see how it ends. If you liked this book, let me know by reviewing or sharing on social media. I love seeing your posts.

If you haven't read the Council series yet, what are you waiting for? Jump in and fall in love with all the gang. You can start here—> Boxset

As usual, this book was made possible because of my lovely PA and bestie, Emma's support. Thank you for everything, you greedy beaver.

Another huge thanks to my Drool MoFo, Megan. Your commentary and assistance help spur me on.

Thanks to Lindsay for being my awesome beta reader and tackling anything I throw at her.

And most of all, to my husband for loving and supporting my crazy dream of writing.

Dangerous Vows

Reckless (Cami's Novella)

Relentless (Nat's Novella)

Dangerous Love

TATTOOED HEARTS DUET

Tattooed Hearts Completed Duet

Riddled Deceit (Part 1)

Smudged Lines (Part 2)

Open Road

VACATION ROMCOM

Vibing

MUSIC CITY DIARIES

Beautiful Agony

SINNERS FAIRYTALES

(standalone)

Pride

About the Author

Kris Butler writes under a pen name to have some separation from her everyday life. Never expecting to write a book, she was surprised when an author friend encouraged her to give it a try and how much she enjoyed it. Having an extensive background in mental health, Kris hopes to normalize mental health issues and the importance of talking about them with her characters and books. Kris is a southern girl at heart but lives with her husband and adorable furbaby somewhere in the Midwest. Kris is an avid fan of Reverse Harem and hopes to add a quirky and new perspective to the emerging genre. If you enjoyed her book, please consider leaving a review. You can contact her the following ways and follow Kris's journey as a new author on social media.

www.ingramcontent.com/pod-product-compliance
Lightning Source LLC
Chambersburg PA
CBHW030802210726
48290CB00002B/387